other books by Jeff Mann

Fiction
A History of Barbed Wire

Poetry
Ash: Poems from Norse Mythology
On the Tongue
Bones Washed with Wine

Essays
Binding the God: Ursine Essays from the Mountain South
Edge: Travels of an Appalachian Leather Bear
Loving Mountains, Loving Men

fog

FOG

A Novel of Desire and Reprisal

Jeff Mann

FOG: A NOVEL OF DESIRE AND REPRISAL

Published in 2011 by Bear Bones Books,
an imprint of Lethe Press, Inc.
118 Heritage Avenue • Maple Shade, NJ 08052-3018
www.lethepressbooks.com • lethepress@aol.com
www.BearBonesBooks.com • bearsoup@gmail.com
ISBN: 1-59021-359-9
ISBN-13: 978-1-59021-359-9

Set in Hoefler Text, Berylium, and Warnock.
Interior design: Alex Jeffers.
Cover artwork/design: Fred Tovich.

acknowledgments

Portions of this novel appeared in *Taken by Force: Erotic Stories of Abduction and Captivity*, edited by Christopher Pierce, and in *Kept Against His Will—Taken by Force Volume II: More Erotic Stories of Abduction and Captivity*, edited by Christopher Pierce.

For Christopher Pierce, Steve Berman, Sven Davisson, and Ron Suresha. Many, many thanks for your ongoing support!

My gratitude as well to Alex Jeffers, who designed the interior, and Fred Tovich, who designed the cover. Thanks for making such a handsome book!

ONE

Life being what it is,
one dreams of revenge.
—Paul Gauguin

chapter one

JANUARY IS THE month of mists. The cove's full of white this morning, making fuzzy shapes of the spruce trees surrounding the house. If I didn't know better, I'd say that someone had plastered the windowpanes with translucent paper, that we were moored inside a pearl. The glass of the pane is frigid beneath my touch. Winter's dedicated to invasions, insisting on its right to enter whom it will.

The fog's pallor continues inside. The pale body on the bed is silent yet, and still, as if carved from cloudy quartz. The only movement this sleeping sculpture makes is the almost imperceptible rise and fall of breath. White, white, wrapped, here and there, in strips of silver-gray.

He's been out for many hours, a chemically induced unconsciousness that's held over two days and several state lines. My fingers still chilled by the windowpane, I bend down and caress his bare belly. Smooth, solid, warm. Skin satiny with youth. I drop to my knees by the bed, kiss his forehead, and suck gently on his hard little nipples.

"Rob," I whisper. "Rob Drake."

No response. I sigh, rise, and settle into a rocking chair to wait. The air is very cold. I'm thankful for my rag wool sweater, the heat of the coffee cup in my hand.

Soon my partner Jay will be home for lunch. Soon Rob will wake. Until then, I want simply to sit here in this silent, fog-swathed house and watch our captive sleep.

JAY DROPS THE Sonic bag on the kitchen table and unpeels his army jacket. His real name's Jeff, but I've learned to call him Jay. Jay and Al: we've been coaching ourselves for a year now, ever since this plan began in earnest, to call one another by pseudonyms. We don't want to give Rob any auditory evidence, in case we decide one day to let him loose, which is a big If. A pit in the forest floor is a more preferable denouement, as far as Jay is concerned.

"Drake still out?" asks Jay.

I nod, dumping out the bag's contents: five containers of tater tots, five foot-longs.

"That extra's for him. Feed him when he comes to."

I nod again. I do a lot of nodding around Jay. Have ever since we met in that D.C. bear bar. Something about his brawny frame, intense eyes, bushy black eyebrows, and deep voice always seems to make him convincing and make me obedient. From ex-con's drinking buddy to ex-con's lover to ex-con's accomplice in a kidnapping. Not the smartest series of moves I've made. Nevertheless, here I am sharing a house with not one but two men I feel passionately about.

Jay and I sit in silence for a good while, chewing on our dogs, before I say, "You know, it's really chilly in here, and I—"

Jay interrupts. He does that a lot, as if trying to spare me from articulating yet another stupid thought. "I want it chilly. I want him to suffer. If you're cold, put on another layer. I want that little shit shaking and whining. No blankets. Don't coddle him, Al. He isn't a guest, he's a captive. You know what his father did. Just 'cause you think he's pretty...okay, I think he's pretty too...but he isn't your sweet boy, he's my tool. Okay?"

"Yes, Jay," I sigh. I need to toughen myself, I know. Jay has reminded me time and time again that Rob deserves what he gets. Sins of the father, and all that.

That's when the noise begins upstairs, behind the thick door of the back bedroom, the ragged cries that Jay's handiwork has so effectively muffled.

Jay grins and takes another bite of his second dog. "Sounds like our boy's up." When I rise, Jay grabs my forearm. "Sit down and finish your lunch. Let him roll around a little and wonder where the hell he is. No one can hear him out here."

As usual, I obey. I sit down and dip a tater tot in ketchup. The noises continue, shouts for help dammed up by rubber and tape. We move to the living room to share one of Jay's hand-rolled cigarettes. "You're right, Al. Sure is cold in here," Jay says. "Maybe tonight we'll start us up a fire." He pulls an afghan over our laps and leans back into the couch's plump pillows. The noises continue, dull thump of a body hitting the floor, bare heels drumming hardwood. Jay puffs out a series of smoke rings and smiles. Mists swirl like curdled silence beneath the spruce. The noises pause, then continue: hapless pounding, stifled cries, glass shattering. "Don't have to be back to work till two today," says Jay, snuffing the cigarette. Stretching out on the couch, his head nestled in my lap, he slips into a nap. I stroke his worn, stubbly, beloved face and listen to Rob's fear. Distant, muted. Sharp edges wrapped in gauze.

chapter two

HALF-HOODS, JUST IN case Rob ever manages to dislodge his blindfold: black leather, with eye-holes. We look pretty frightening in them, and, as Jay likes to point out, fright is what this foray into abduction is all about. Our prisoner's yelled and thrashed on and off through Jay's lengthy nap, but the silence prevailing now behind the padlocked back bedroom door indicates that he's worn himself out.

Jay unlocks the door and eases it open. Rob's no longer on the bare mattress where we left him. He's lying on the floor on his side, blindfolded and gagged, bound hand and foot, back against the far wall. His chest's heaving, his head's raised and cocked toward the sound of our entrance. Signs of his struggle scatter the room: mussed throw rugs, a tipped-over chair, a shattered lamp.

"Here's our boy," Jay says sweetly. "Active little shit, aren't you? Broke a lamp too." He rights the furniture, then strides over and, without a word of warning, kicks Rob in the gut with his steel-toed work boot.

Rob gasps, rolls away, and curses.

"Shut up, boy," Jay snarls, kicking him a second time. Rob curls up into a ball like a sowbug, groaning.

"Jay, don't—" I begin, but as usual Jay cuts in, this time with "I'll treat him any goddamn way I want." He presses his boot sole into the side of Rob's face, then growls, "Get over here and help me get this little fucker back on the bed."

As soon as we touch Rob, he starts thrashing. He's six feet tall and pretty much all muscle, so he's a load, but Jay and I are both bigger and broader, and soon enough, despite our prisoner's vigorous struggles, we've dumped him onto the bed on his back. He's screaming again, but the sound doesn't seem to please Jay any longer. Rob's disobeying an express order to shut up, and Jay gets very angry when folks don't do what they're told. Pulling out his army dagger, Jay straddles Rob's chest and holds the blade to the straining chords of his throat.

"Okay, kid, that's enough," Jay hisses through gritted teeth. "I've had enough of your noise now. Fun's over. Shut up and keep still, or I'll cut you bad. I've gotten this blade mighty sharp just for you."

Rob's young—twenty-two—but he's not stupid. Suddenly he's as unmoving as he was while unconscious, once again that fog-pale statue.

"Good boy," Jay grunts, patting Rob's cheek with the flat of the blade, then climbing off him. "Watch him, Al. I'll be right back. Gotta fetch something from the basement."

I wait till I can no longer hear the tromp of Jay's boot soles before I touch Rob. When I grasp his shoulder, he jumps with fright.

"I'm not going to hurt you," I say softly. "I'm going to roll you over onto your side so your hands won't go numb. Okay?"

Rob lies there panting. He's obviously suspicious of my concern after the brutal treatment he just got. But then he nods and I ease him over.

He doesn't resist as I squeeze his fingers to check his circulation. They're warm, not cold; pink, not purplish. All good signs. Jay's an expert.

"I'll bet you're hungry, right?"

Rob nods.

"I'll feed you once he leaves. You need to use the bathroom, I suspect."

Another wordless affirmative, this one more urgent.

"Okay, once he leaves."

There's a heavy tread on the stairs and the clinking of metal. Jay appears in the door, grim-faced, with an armful of chain.

chapter three

AFTERNOON RAIN'S REPLACED the morning fog. The wind's brisk, blowing sheets of wet against the glass. We thought about boarding up the windows in this room, but Jay decided that we were too far up the cove for anyone to hear anything as long as we kept Rob gagged. I sit in my chair, masked in black, rocking, sipping more coffee, studying our prisoner's pale body. Jay's ordered me to watch him, and that's a job I'm more than willing to take. I need to feed him in a minute, but first I want to take his youth and loveliness in, this boy I've come to care for despite my better judgment.

Rob lies where Jay left him, on the broad bed. His hands are duct-taped behind his back. Several lengths of tape are wrapped around his bare torso and upper arms; another strip of tape secures his elbows together. More tape binds his ankles. The big rubber ball filling his mouth is held in place with another few feet of tape we've wrapped around his head. To make sure he never sees our faces, there's a good bit of tape plastered over his eyes. The latest addition to these safeguards is the short, heavy chain Jay just padlocked around both Rob's neck and the headboard, to insure that he doesn't range off the bed and rearrange the furniture again. In other words, our captive's going nowhere. Jay's seen to that. He has no intention of seeing his revenge short-circuited after waiting so long for it.

The strips of silver-gray tape are wrapped around a physique of remarkable beauty. Rob's nearly naked. He's got nothing on but white briefs, his sweatshirt, running shorts, and tennis shoes having been removed once we had him drugged in the back of the van. This exposure serves several functions. He suffers from the cold; his sense of vulnerability and humiliation is intensified. Best of all, we can see the fine lines of his body, an athletic build shaped by years of gymnastics, as well as weightlifting and jogging the boy's been dedicated to lately in preparation for the police academy. I know all this about him and more, having spied on Rob for a long while now in preparation for his abduction.

His shoulders are very broad, his hips narrow and lean. His chest's hard and curved, like a Roman breastplate, and smooth, save for the brown hairs rimming his small cold-stiff nipples. The upper arms taped to his torso are lined with well-defined muscles that bulge and relax as he flexes them, silently and futilely, against the tape. His belly is flat, ridged, and hairless; a light line of fur begins below his navel and disappears into his underwear. His legs are as muscular as his torso, but, in contrast to his upper body, very, very hairy.

Right now he's lying on his side facing me, but I know—having cut clothes off him, having studied his bound and sleeping form over the hundreds of miles we've driven, having helped Jay lug him up here to this cold room in this remote cove—that the forearms bound behind his back are coated with golden-brown hair; his buttocks are firm, white, smooth, and dimpled with regular athletic exertion; the cleft between is fuzzy with brown fur; and there's an extensive tattoo on his back, deep black dramatic against his skin's white, a ladder of tribal spikes and swirls that begins at his waist, climbs his spine, and covers his upper back like black fire, flickering over his hard lats and curling to an end over his shoulders and the nape of his neck.

His face? Well, that's pretty much concealed by the tape that gags and blindfolds him. But I know his handsome features regardless. I've come to dote on his friendly, trusting blue eyes, his long, straight nose, his thin lips occasionally pursed with thought but more often smiling, his chin occasionally shaved smooth but more often stubbly with a goatee that never quite gets there before he shaves it off again. Right now his chin and jaw are covered with a two-day growth of beard—we took him on Tuesday and today is Thursday—and I rub the roughness of it now before unlocking the chain around his neck, sitting him up on the edge of the bed, and peeling the tape off his mouth.

The ball is very big and so his jaw must be very sore: he can't spit it out by himself, though he tries. I curve a finger into the side of his mouth and around the ball, then gently dislodge it. Rob gasps, and a little pool of built-up saliva dribbles over his lips and onto his chin. He works his jaw around, and I massage his face till he begins to speak.

The voice I recognize from my careful stalkings. I've sat near him in restaurants and coffee shops for months now, listening to his conversations both face to face and via cell phone. It's youthful and deep, but the usual jovial, macho, hearty tone—boy doing his best to be a man—has been entirely banished by his situation. Now his voice is trembling, a wet quiver. The change both disturbs and delights me. It's thrilling and saddening to see manliness so shaken, so broken down.

"Where am I? Why are you doing this to me?" Rob says, licking his lips. Stupidly, abruptly, he tries to stand, but his ankles are taped tightly together and he almost falls. Wrapping an arm around his shoulders, I force him back down onto the bed.

"Careful, or you'll hurt yourself. If you promise to behave, I'll tell you what's up," I say, trying to sound as determined and ruthless as Jay actually is. What I've got to fight back right now is the strong urge to take this scared boy in my arms and comfort him. "I took the gag out to feed you lunch, but you start making noise, the ball gets taped back in, all right?"

Rob nods. I hold him against me, steadying him. Goose-pimpled alabaster. Michelangelo's David wrapped in the tight anachronism of duct tape. He's shaking violently. I reach up and ruffle his short brown buzz-cut as if I were his gymnastics coach encouraging him back onto the rings.

What can I tell him? Nothing solid, for any of those facts would reveal our identities and motives and thus doom him. Ignorant, he has a good chance, after we use him, of being found by authorities in a roadside ditch, bound, gagged, but still alive. Aware of Jay's reasons for revenge, he's guaranteed a shallow grave.

So I lie, hoping that I sound convincing. "Look, kid, you know how a kidnapping works. We've contacted your father and asked for a ransom. While we wait for that to be delivered, we're going to hold you here. Sorry if you're uncomfortable. We'll need to keep you bound and gagged till you're freed; it's a necessary precaution. The ransom should come through in a couple of days, a week at the most. As long as you keep quiet, don't fight us, and do what you're told, I promise you that you won't be hurt. Once the money shows, we'll take you home. If you do fight us, well, my partner is pretty vicious, so I suspect you'll end up damaged or worse. Understand?"

"Y-yeah. Okay." Rob nods feebly. His quivering lips firm up. "I won't give you any trouble," he mutters, his shaky voice growing steadier. "I'll do whatever you say. Just don't hurt me, okay, dude?"

"'Dude?' Very cute. I forget how young you are," I say, retrieving the Sonic bag from the bedside table. He's taking it all pretty well, considering the traumatic circumstances. No surprise, really. The boy's an athlete, working on a degree in criminal investigations, hoping to follow in his father's law-enforcement footsteps, all of which means that he's deeply invested in traditional American concepts of manhood, and that means being brave, strong, and stoic in the face of danger. He takes what answers I give without pleading for more information, his trembling subsides, he chomps on the hot dog and tater tots I hold to his mouth, gulps two glasses of water, and thanks me. When I cut his feet loose and walk him to the bathroom, he thanks me again. He doesn't protest when I pull his briefs down—small, fright-limp penis in a fluff of brown hair, muscles of his lean loins shaped like Apollo's lyre—and when I gently push him onto the toilet seat to do some long-delayed business. He doesn't even complain when I wipe his ass, though a deep red flush spreads over his pale features.

I suspect this admirable stoicism is about to break down, however. Now that I have Rob bare-assed in the bathroom, it's time to explain what I must do next, what Jay's ordered me to do, and I dread the boy's reaction.

"Okay, son. You need to bend over. I've got to clean you out." What I'm holding in my hand, what my hostage can't see, is called an anal spike: a rubber sphere soon to be filled with warm water that I'll squirt up Rob's ass so as to ready him for a good plowing. I've used it for years to prepare myself for Jay's enthusiastic cock-thrusts; now it's Rob's turn.

"What? Clean me out? What'd you mean?"

"Your ass, kid. This won't hurt. It's just water. I'm just going to squirt it up inside you."

"But why?" The quiver's returned to Rob's voice.

"Jay told me to. For...later tonight. Once he gets home, he's going to..." As often as I've fantasized about it, I can't bring myself to say it.

"What? What's he going to do tonight? What—? Oh, no!" That's when Rob starts begging: when he realizes that his body is not only going to be kept immobile but also used. "Please, oh man, please, no. Don't! Don't let him! Don't let him do that!"

His pleas break my heart and stiffen my dick. Panicked, he starts to struggle, staggering blindly against me, fighting my grip. "Help! Help, somebody!" he shouts. "Jesus, somebody help me!"

"Shut up, you stupid boy! There's no one around to hear you. Just shut up!"

"Don't let him! God! Please! Help!"

"Shut *up*!" I snarl. Seizing a moist washcloth from the shower stall, I ball it up and force it into Rob's mouth. The din continues nonetheless, albeit muffled now. "UHHM!! Hhmmm!" the boy shouts, thrashing about in my grasp.

"Kid, stop it!" Gripping his throat, I slam him against the wall and clamp a hand over his mouth. "Stop fighting and shut up! I'll fetch Jay's knife if you don't stop. You hear me? You hear me? Shut up," I hiss, "or I swear I'll carve you up."

The threat works: Rob abruptly stops his noisy struggle.

"You gonna obey me now?"

Rob whimpers, nods, and sags against me.

"That's a good boy. Keep that rag in your mouth, try to relax, and just take this," I growl. "It won't hurt. It's just a little plastic tube and some warm water."

Shoving him onto his knees, I bend him over till his face is pressed against the floor and his ass is angled up. I fill the sphere, lube up the plastic tip, spread his buttocks, and, as gently as possible, slide the thin tube up Rob's asshole. He winces and shakes his head. "Na! Naa!" His pleading soaks the washrag, an amalgam of humiliation and desperation I do my best to ignore. Three times I squirt him full, order him to hold it in, sit him on the toilet, order him to release, before finally cleaning him up with another washrag, lifting him to his feet, and pulling his briefs back on.

I'm about to lead him back to the bedroom when I see the streaks gleaming on his pallid cheeks. Tears are trickling from beneath his tape blindfold. When I pull the washrag out of his mouth, he starts to sob.

"Ah, kid..." I groan, gripping his shoulder, steadying his blindness, what little anger left in me fading fast. Having something pushed up his ass has made what's to come tonight far too real.

"Please don't!" Rob bawls. "Jesus, man, I have a girlfriend. Don't rape me! Don't let him rape me! Please!"

Pity feels like a jagged rock caught in my windpipe. I can't help but hug him. I wrap my arms around him and let him sob. Standing there in the bright light of the bathroom, anal spike in the sink, lube on the back of the toilet, the nigh-nude young man I've helped to kidnap presses against me, weeping wildly. His face nestles against my shoulder, wetting the wool with his frightened boy's tears. He's still crying as I lead him back to the bedroom, tape his ankles together, and help him onto the mattress. He rolls into a fetal position, sides shaking.

"Kid, stop, please." Now it's my turn to beg. I stroke his shoulder, pat his head awkwardly, say stupid things like "Jay's determined to do this, I can't tell you why, I can't stop him," and "I'll be here tonight, I'll try to get him to go slow, so it doesn't hurt too bad."

If only Jay weren't so strong, if only I weren't so weak, if only Rob's father hadn't answered that APB so long ago. The boy's so handsome and pitiable with tape over his eyes, tears sliding down his stubbled cheeks. My attempts at being ruthless haven't worked too well, and now I give entirely into the tender ache his beauty and helplessness ignite in me. I climb onto the bed, wrap an arm around Rob's waist, snuggle up against him, his heaving back against my chest, and hold him until his tears are done.

As soon as Rob stops crying, he starts to shiver, a full-body quake. The fear I can't do much about. The cold I can, despite what I promised Jay. What he doesn't know won't hurt anyone. I rise, cross the room, open the closet, and soon enough I'm soothing Rob beneath a flannel sheet and a heavy comforter, our heads resting on the same pillow.

"Better?" I ask, hugging him close, warming him up, and Rob whispers, "Yes." I wipe the wet off his cheeks, and Rob whispers, "Thanks, dude." He curls uncomplaining against my chest, acquiescent, accepting my affection, thankful, I suppose, for any kindness he can get.

"I'm going to have to gag you again before he comes home, and I'm going to have to put these blankets away. Understand?"

Rob nods.

"Don't tell him I let you get warm, all right?"

"I get it," Rob says. He's still shivering, so I pull him closer. He feels very, very sweet. Holding him feels like honey tastes. Our bodies fit together as nicely as I've always thought they would, ever since I started following him on Jay's instructions. I'd love to fondle his nipples and cock right now, but that might frighten him, so I refrain. Now that I'm holding him this close, I want inside him as badly as Jay does. I only hope he can't feel my hard-on beneath my pants.

"I'll do my best tonight, but you've got to face facts. Jay's going to do what he wants with you, and neither of us can do anything about it. He's my partner. He's older, stronger, wiser.

I owe him a lot. I do what he says. He's been planning your abduction for a long time."

Rob swallows hard but says nothing.

"Try not to cry tonight. Weakness only makes him meaner. Just lie still as best you can and try to keep quiet."

Rob nods. We lie there together listening to rain drip off the eaves and patter the windows. Exhausted from terror and struggle, knowing instinctively that he's safe with me, Rob falls asleep in my arms. I stroke his face, kiss his tattooed shoulders, the fine hairs on the nape of his neck. He's young enough to be my son.

I watch the clock on the wall. Two hours pass; afternoon's gray light dwindles. Half an hour before Jay's due home, I wake Rob, push the ball back into his mouth, tape it in, chain his neck to the bed frame, and return the bedclothes and pillow to the closet. I head downstairs to wait for Jay, leaving Rob alone to quake in the cold and the dark.

chapter four

GLOOMY DUSK BY the time Jay gets home from the sawmill. He has lots of buddies in this little mountain town, and, thanks to them, he makes a decent living through odd jobs paid under the table, which I supplement with my online work sorting medical records. Tonight, we have a few bottles of beer with the pizza he picked up. We watch the news. By now, Rob's been reported missing, but we're barely worried. We're many states away now; we've left no clues. Jay's pretty much a legal non-entity, thanks to some ex-con friends of his who are computer hackers. No way Rob's father or the authorities could connect the kidnapping to Jay, much less track him down.

It's rain-gusty dark when Jay decides it's time. He turns up the thermostat. He puts out his cigarette, grabs another beer, takes a long swig, and heads up the stairs. I follow. When we pass the bathroom, I stop Jay long enough to point to the anal spike in the sink as proof of my obedience and to grab the tube of lube.

fog

Jay brushes a lock of hair out of his eyes, takes another gulp of beer, and grins at me. I love him so much. I understand why he's doing what he's doing. Rob's father was the cop who wounded Jay, who shot Jay's first lover to death, during that armed robbery attempt. Officer Drake's testimony sent Jay to prison for nearly a decade. He's lost so much, suffered so much. Things need righted. If only Rob weren't so young, so tender, so innocent. Why does suffering have to be a black wind-borne seed sprouting more of the same?

"What's that goo for?" says Jay with a crooked grin, gazing blankly at the lube.

"You know, when you... You know he's got to be a virgin. You'll need lots of...you'll need to..."

Jay's grin broadens with the glee he only displays when someone he hates is soon to be in pain. He's been waiting for this evening for nine years. Rob was thirteen when Jay went to prison and this hate began. "I don't need lube. I've got this," he says, hawking a glob of spittle into his hand. "And if he's too tight, I got this," he says, taking one last swig and holding up the empty beer bottle. Guffawing, he strokes the long neck of brown glass. Handing me the bottle, he reaches into a back pants pocket, pulls out his mask, and pulls it over his face; from a front pocket he pulls out his key ring and unlocks the padlock on the bedroom door.

"You still don't get it, baby. I want him to hurt. For his father's sake. Now get your party mask on. I'm ready to celebrate. Fuuuuck, this is gonna be fun!"

I hand the beer bottle back to Jay and pull black leather over my head. The door swings open. The hallway light falls across the figure curled up on the bed. Rob's lying on his side, fetal, frightened, facing us. Beneath the tape blindfold, his blue eyes, I know, are full of animal panic, wet and wild.

"Light some candles, Al. I want this to be romantic," Jay says. He sets the beer bottle on the floor by the bed, then sits in the rocking chair long enough to unlace his work boots and tug them off. Standing, he peels off his jeans and boxers, pulls his sweatshirt and undershirt over his head, then from the pile of clothing retrieves his army knife from its sheath on his belt. He stands before me smiling in candlelight, naked save for boot socks and hood, thick erection bobbing and swaying eagerly before him, knife in his right hand. With his muscle-bound build, the thick dark pelt carpeting his chest and belly, the sharp blade, and the black hood, he looks like a magnificent and entirely fearsome executioner. I'm glad that Rob's blindfolded, because if he saw the man about to take him, he'd probably piss the bed. My response to Jay's sinister nakedness is one entirely different from what Rob's might have been, however: my cock grows stiff in my jeans. "Take it easy on him," I say, gripping Jay's arm, my eyes roaming over his brawny body. Jay's hotter than anyone I've ever known. Every time I see him naked, any doubts I have about him dissolve like morning fog, and every crazy thing I've done to please him makes sudden sense.

Jay laughs, shakes off my hand, and sits beside Rob on the bed. "Sure is chilly in here, Al, but here's a little man who can warm us up." He strokes the strips of tape over our captive's face and tugs at the chain anchoring his neck to the headboard. "You're a pretty sexy little guy, aren't you? Built like a brick shithouse, that's for sure." Shaking his head admiringly, he runs his hand over Rob's bare pecs, flicking a nipple. "I got something for you, pretty boy. It's been a long time coming." He grips the flesh of Rob's ass and squeezes roughly.

Rob shakes his head and starts begging. Despite the tape and the rubber ball, the intonation makes it clear that what he's murmuring over and over again is "Please." Rob's still begging and shaking his head as Jay warns, "I won't tolerate any fight, kid. Remember I have a knife. And if you thrash around too much, you'll choke yourself on that chain." He's still begging and shaking his head as Jay rolls him onto his belly and with the tip of the dagger traces the tattooed flames in the small of Rob's back.

"Shut up and keep still. I need to get you naked," says Jay. Rob obeys, save for a fine panting and shivering obviously beyond his control. Slipping the knife between Rob's left thigh and his briefs, Jay slides steel through cloth, severing the waistband, then does the same with the right side. Together, we tug the tatters of cloth off Rob's loins, baring his buttocks.

Our sigh is simultaneous. There's something ritualistic, faintly religious about this. Funny phrases from my church-going childhood run through my mind. *Penetralia, tabernacle, holy of holies, the rending of the veil.*

"Holy shit, you're fine," Jay hisses, stroking Rob's exposed ass with the flat of the blade. "This is going to be even sweeter than I thought."

Jay rests the bare knife on Rob's back, between his taped triceps, in the shallow valley between his shoulder blades, sharp silvery glitter nested in swirls of tattooed black flame. "That's razor sharp, kid, so lie real still now," Jay warns. Straddling Rob's thighs, with a fingertip Jay brushes the cleft between his buttocks, curls of brown fur between smooth curves of white. Bending, he brushes his stubble-rough chin over each trembling cheek. He wets a forefinger in his mouth, slides it between Rob's buttocks, and ranges enthusiastically, as if trying to uncover a buried jewel.

Rob gasps into his gag. Jay grins—"Ah, here we are!"—and probes for a while. "Ummmmmm, sweet! So sweet and tight!" He smiles at me, licking his lips. I've never seen him happier.

"You need to open up, boy. If you don't, I got a longneck with your butt-hole's name on it."

Rob yelps and jerks as Jay burrows deeper. His shoulders stiffen, the muscles of his arms tense and flex, fighting the tight grip of the duct tape that binds them. I fall to my knees by the bed and fondle Rob's face. "Poor boy," I murmur. His unshaven cheeks are moist again, but he's taking my advice, for this time his weeping is not violent but silent.

"Easy, easy," I whisper, smoothing temples wet with fear-sweat. "Keep quiet. Try to relax." As if relaxation in the face of rape would ever be possible. Rob nods beneath my hand. He gulps, breathes deeply, and falls limp. The mattress beneath his face is darkening with tears.

"Yeah, comfort him, Al. We're like a pair of angels, huh? You be the comforter, I'll be the avenger," Jay growls. He pulls his finger out, spits between Rob's buttocks, and recommences his exploration.

Jay's probing, I'm caressing, Rob's wincing and quietly panting for a good while before Jay's had enough of this reconnoitering. "Got a finger in," Jay announces triumphantly. "A good start." Lifting the dagger off Rob's back, he climbs off the bed, slices the tape off our prisoner's ankles, and nudges his hairy thighs apart. He runs the dull edge of the blade along the fuzzy thicket of Rob's ass-crack, eliciting goose pimples and suppressed sobs.

Smiling, Jay looks up from his knife-play long enough to lob a few orders my way. "Al, baby, fetch a pillow from the closet. I want to prop his butt up at a nice angle. Then grab an old sheet and some towels to roll out beneath him. If he bleeds, I don't want this mattress stained. And get that rope in the bureau's bottom drawer. We'll need to rope his ankles to the bedposts. I want his legs spread nice and wide."

chapter five

I KNOW WHAT Rob will be feeling. At least some of it. I know that hairy, heavy weight on top of me, Jay's rough chin chafing the back of my neck, his hand clamped over my mouth, his thick cock shoving in and out of me. I'm addicted to that feeling. It's one of the reasons I've done what I've done to stay with Jay. I spread my legs willingly; I open my well-lubed hole and rear back against him. I moan against the sweaty pressure of his palm, begging him to spear me harder. I love Jay's cock up my ass, his hips heaving into me, his low growls filling my ears as he cums inside me.

Rob's pillow-propped, spread and tied, just the way Jay wants him. But Jay's cock is too big and eager, Rob's hole's too tight and terrified. After a few unsuccessful attempts to push his thick dick inside, Jay smears the neck of the beer bottle with spit, just as he'd threatened. Again, I beg him to use lube; again, he refuses.

"Open up, goddamn you," he snarls, sliding the makeshift dildo between Rob's ass cheeks. The bottleneck jabs against resistance. Rob whimpers. Jay lifts the bottle to his mouth and deep-throats it, coating it with more saliva, then tries again. Rob's thighs strain—attempt to thrash his legs, cut short by the ropes binding his feet—his taped hands fumble air, and the bottle slides halfway in. Rob throws his head back, then slumps against the mattress. Jay grins, pushes, and the bottleneck disappears inside. Rob jerks violently, the chain around his neck rattles. Jay pulls the bottle completely out, then slowly pushes in again. Rob's buttocks clench; he emits a long, low groan. Jay begins a rhythm, slow at first, then quickening. Still on my knees by the bed, I stroke Rob's slick forehead. My hands are trembling; my dick is stiff. Rain slams the windowpane in torrents, makes drumming music on the tin roof.

What I have known, groaning beneath Jay during our years together, is consensual passion, not fear and pain. My face contorts with ecstasy, not agony, when Jay enters me. This long-awaited night, as the bottle slides in and out, Rob's face, what parts of it the tape isn't concealing, twists with something I've never felt. He's beyond my touch now, my attempts to comfort. His brow is furrowed, his jaw set. Beneath my futile fingers, sweat rolls off his scalp. Each time the bottle's driven home, his fists clench, his head tosses like a storm-swallowed treetop.

"Good boy. All opened up for Daddy," sighs Jay. "And no blood either. So far."

Pulling out the bottle, he lays it on the floor on its side, where it rolls noisily across the wood till a carpet stops its progress. "Hold him down, Al," Jay orders.

A sheet of rain rattles the window. I climb onto the bed, stretch out on my side beside Rob, and drape an arm over his shoulders, my face close to his. "You'll be all right, kid," I say, caressing his wet brow and the tape over his mouth. "Just try to open up, so it won't hurt so much."

"Hmmm mmm," Rob manages, nodding beneath my touch.

"Jay, please be easy on him. I'm begging you. You know we can't take him to the hospital if—"

"We'll see how it goes," Jay says, winking at me. "Depends on whether he acts like a man or a cry-baby." He kisses our prisoner's right buttock, then his left. He moistens his meat and Rob's hole with another palmful of spit, then rolls on top of him. Rob breathes hard through his nose as his abductor's furry heft crushes him into the bed. Jay nuzzles Rob's neck and cheek, just as he does mine when he's about to ride me, just as tenderly.

"Here we go, kid," he whispers, reaching beneath to position the head of his cock just right. "You gonna keep quiet for me?"

Rob hesitates, then nods. Jay wipes the wet off Rob's cheek, licks tear-salt from his fingers, and whispers, "You gonna take it like a big boy? Gonna stop crying?"

Rob hesitates, then nods. This time it's a firm, determined gesture, suddenly nothing of the quaking adolescent left in his demeanor. "Good boy!" Jay says, all triumph, proud as a doting parent, wrapping his arms tightly around Rob's torso and kissing his buzz-cut.

Rob does what he's been told—no sobs, no screams—as Jay's cock slowly slides up his ass. Why Jay's taking him so slowly, I don't know. I figured he'd shove the whole thing in with one thrust to insure the greatest pain possible. But now, weirdly, Jay seems to have caught some of my compassion. Or maybe he's just rewarding Rob's obedience or show of strength. Whatever it is, I'm relieved. I was expecting screams and blood all evening. Instead, Rob lies there, panting quietly, as Jay's thick dick fills him up. Jay even waits a minute or two to let our captive's hole grow somewhat accustomed to its fleshy invader before he starts a regular thrusting.

Rob hisses, falls silent, grunts, falls silent, gulps, falls silent. The storm outside continues its siege. I kiss Rob's forehead, hugging him to me. Jay sighs and gasps, "Jesus, oh Jesus." The candle flames shiver and leap. Jay rides Rob's pale ass, in and out, in and out. Jay grins over at me, pecks my cheek, and grunts, "God damn, Al, you gotta get some of this." The bed creaks like sailboats in a windy harbor. The men upon the bed rock like sailboats on a rough sea, up and down, forward and back, forward and back, and I am a dingy in their wake.

This goes on a long time, a length I gauge by the tightness in my heart, the hard lump in my jeans, and the dwindling height of the candles. Then Rob's pleas start up again. He shakes his head and starts to struggle, twisting his torso within Jay's embrace. By now he must be really starting to hurt, and so his bravery's quickly eroding.

Jay's response to this feeble protest is in character. "Shut up," he mutters, cocking an arm firmly around Rob's neck. "Shut the fuck up." The taped-tight pleading turns to whimpers. The whimpers grade into small choking sounds, soft snorts, as Jay slowly cuts off Rob's breath.

"Jesus, don't kill him," I say.

"Hand me the knife," Jay says. Without thought I fetch the dagger from the floor where Jay had tossed it. Jay claps one hand over Rob's mouth and presses the blade to his throat.

"By God, you be quiet now, or I'll cut you bad."

One touch of the steel, and Rob's pleading and straining instantly stop. His fight wilts. He goes limp, utterly silent, lean hips bouncing beneath his rapist's thrusts.

Jay's angry now. His speed and rhythm are savage now, all mercy abandoned. Rougher and rougher seas. The headboard starts slamming the wall; the chain links clink.

"You like this, right? Tell me you like it, boy," Jay pants, sliding the knife over Rob's throat.

The tears have started again. I can see their sheen in the candlelight.

"Tell me, boy."

Rob gulps and nods, a very small nod, almost imperceptible, the knowledge of steel cold and sharp against his skin.

"Tell me you want more, boy," Jay pants. He flicks his wrist. Rob yelps. I don't have to see blood to know Jay's cut him.

"Jay!" I'm ready at last to push him off, to wrestle the knife away, to stop this cruelty.

"Just a nick, lover." He gazes up at me, winks again, then returns his attention to the bound and naked body pitching helplessly beneath him.

"Tell me you need more of this. Tell me you can't get enough of being plowed. Tell me you've waited all your life for this. Tell me you're my bitch. Tell me you're my little boy-cunt, my sweet little cum-dump. Beg me to fuck you harder." Jay pounds into him, faster and deeper, knife still held to his throat, hand still clamped over his taped mouth.

The headboard clatters, the slave-chain rattles, the bound boy hums. "Mmmm mm MMM. Mmmm mmm MMMM. Mmm mmm MMMM." The musical accents of Rob's gagged moans match my lover's cock-thrusts. A slave's stifled acquiescence—it makes my dick leak. I squeeze Rob's shoulder and tug on my crotch simultaneously. Suddenly I know, as much as I love being Jay's bottom, I've been wanting a beautiful slave like Rob all my life.

"Say, 'Please give me more, Sir.'" Jay's voice is shaky. I can tell he's on the edge. "Say, 'Please cum up my hole, Sir.'"

"Mmm mm mmm, mmm mm MMM, mmm mm MMM, mmm mm MMM." It rocks like a melodic phrase, like a baby's cradle.

"Tighten your ass around my dick, boy," Jay growls. "Squeeze my dick dry, bitch, or I'll cut you again."

Rob bows his head, lifts his ass, and bucks back against Jay's thrusts. Jay shouts, "Oh, fuck, yeah! Oh, fuck, yeah, that's sweet! Yeah, that's right! Yeah!" buries his cock to the hilt, stiffens, shudders, and collapses.

AS SOON AS I free his feet, Rob tucks into his customary fetal position and passes out from pain, terror, and exhaustion. Jay curls up beside him, worn out with consummated hatred and delight, smiling drowsily. Soon they're both asleep, Jay's thick arm sprawled over Rob, his face pressed against Rob's tattooed back.

I bend down to kiss Jay's unshaven cheek, to kiss Rob's unshaven chin. I touch the dried blood on his neck, softly, reverently, and on the sheet beneath him, as if the red-brown smears were saints' relics. For a moment, I listen to the continuing batter of rain on the roof. Then I strip, blow out the candles, and fetch blankets from the closet. I cover the sleepers, then slip in beside them, nestling Rob between us. I wrap my arms around Rob, reach over him to stroke Jay's face. I fight off slumber for a good while, lying here, listening to the storm's turmoil, listening to my lovers' soft snores.

Yes, somehow I love them both. Somehow I will save them both. Somehow, through some miracle not yet comprehended or conceived, I will save us all.

chapter six

WHEN I WAKE to gray morning, Jay's gone. 9:10 says the bedside clock. He's already at work at the sawmill. Outside there's the caw of crows, ragged and rhythmic, in the spruce trees; on the roof is the shushing sound of soft rain.

Our captive's huddled on his side, back to me, on the far side of the bed, one white shoulder exposed to the chill. When I touch that muscled skin, he jumps and whimpers; he shakes his head.

"Don't be afraid, kid," I say, sliding across the bed, pressing my nakedness against his—my chest to his inked back and bound arms, my crotch to his butt, the front of my thighs to the back of his legs. I adjust the blankets over us, slip an arm beneath his head, and wrap another around his well-taped torso.

"*Huh* uh. *Huh* uh!" Rob grunts. He's tense and trembling again, no doubt anticipating further brutality. It's to be expected, this fear of touch, the morning after a rape. Thanks to all that time in prison, it took Jay months before he could relax beneath my hands and tongue. Months, and a lot of beer every night, a habit I've learned to share with him.

"I'm going to hold you whether you want me to not. There's nothing you can do about it, right?"

The boy's entirely robbed of will, and he knows it. He gives a weak nod, giving me no trouble as I stroke his face and fondle his nipples. When I nudge a thumb between his ass cheeks and find the wet hole there, he emits a choked sob.

"I'm not going to do what Jay did. Yet. Are you hurting here?"

Rob nods. His ass-cheeks clench against my hand.

"Ah, poor kid," I sigh, bending over to kiss a buttock. It's like a snow-covered hill, but warm, the skin so soft, the underlying muscle firm with athleticism and youth. "No surprise. Jay pounded you pretty hard. You were a virgin there, right?"

Rob manages a weak nod and another choked sob.

"At least he opened you up with that bottle. He took his time at first. It could have been a lot worse. How bad you hurting? Real bad?"

"Mm uh." Rob shakes his head. "Mm uhg."

"Not so bad? That's good. To be honest, I expected blood. He was a lot easier on you than I thought he'd be. Jay can be pretty damned savage." Gently I stroke the little orifice Jay ravaged last night. The hair surrounding it is long and silky. How badly I want to jam a couple of fingers up inside our sweet hostage, lube us up, hoist his legs over my shoulders, shove in my cock, and use him the way Jay did last night. Part of me wants to make this boy bruise, bleed, and sob, and part of me wants to soothe him and care for him. The typically complex yearnings of thc kinkily queer. During our several leather-sex years together, Jay's taught me that. "Am I hurting you now?"

"Hm uh. Naa."

"Good." I pat his hip. "You ready for the toilet and then some breakfast?"

Rob nods.

"I'll allow you both if you try to relax and cuddle closer to me."

Hesitation, then obedience. Rob scoots back against me. He takes a series of deep, deliberate breaths through his nose. Slowly his body loses its tension; slowly his quaking subsides.

"Good boy. You see how painless things can be if you do what you're told? I'll take your gag out now if you promise to keep quiet. All right?"

When Rob nods, I peel off the several feet of tape plastered over his mouth and wrapped around his head. He moans with discomfort as the last layer comes off, tugging at his stubbly beginnings of a beard and the hair on the back of his neck. "UH!" he gasps as I remove the ball. As before, drool gushes over his chin. I wipe it off with the back of my hand.

"Messy boy." I chuckle. "What do you say?"

"Thanks, dude," he mumbles.

"I'm tired of this sweaty mask," I say, peeling it off and tossing it atop the bedside table. "Don't try to work your blindfold off, okay? If you see my face, well, to be blunt, I'll have to shoot you through the head."

"Oh, Jesus," Rob gasps. "I'm not crazy. I want to live. I won't fool with the blindfold, I swear to God. Just don't hurt me."

"Right answer. Up we go." I haul Rob off the bed and to his feet. Stiffly he shuffles beside me down the hall. Halfway there, he stops.

"Oh. Oh, God." He leans forward slightly. There's a wet popping sound. I look down to find the thick ooze of Jay's semen sliding down the back of Rob's thighs.

"Oh," he says again, as if he'd forgotten something important. I pat his taped-down biceps. His face is as red as a tulip. "Come on. I'll clean you up."

In the bathroom, I wipe the semen away, then help Rob piss, his limp cock in my hand. Next, he sits on the toilet. His face knots up as he relieves himself further.

"Hurts, huh?"

"Yeah," Rob whispers, head bowed. He strains, giving half-audible whimpers.

"Yeah, if you're not used to getting fucked, and even if you are, sometimes..."

I give him a few more moments. "Done?"

"Yeah." His forehead is flushed, a deep crimson. He reminds me, absurdly, of a McIntosh apple, red atop snow-white.

I lift him up, bend him over, and wipe him clean. He could be a wounded soldier, and I his nurse.

"Thank you," Rob says, a fine tremble threading his voice. Right now he's the embodiment of masculine shame. It's delicious.

"Come on, boy." Down the stairs we go, Rob's every wince and awkward movement evincing his discomfort after last night's brutal use. In the kitchen I put a cushion on a chair to make sitting easier, slide him onto it, and shawl him with an afghan before pouring out two cups of coffee from the pot Jay's made earlier.

"Welcome to the Mountain Hideaway Hotel. How you like your coffee?"

"Uh. Just some sugar. Please."

I mix it up, taking a sip to gauge its heat, then hold it to his lips. He slurps. "Thank you," he whispers again.

"You city boys have more manners than I would have expected. Did you get some sleep?"

"On and off. It's really hard to get comfortable taped up like this. My shoulders are killing me. Any way you could let me loose for a while? Or just loosen my bonds some? I won't try to get away, I promise."

"Yeah, yeah. Sounding like a ploy to me, kid. Not just yet. Sorry. How about some breakfast? Ever had scrapple? It's kind of a redneck breakfast, but it's tasty, especially with fried eggs on top. Just shredded pork with cornmeal. Kinda like corn mush."

"Scrapple? No, I haven't heard of that." Rob bites his lip and lifts his head. "Redneck, huh? Are you a redneck? Al? That's your name, right? Smells like redneck in here. Musty. Cold. Trashy."

All right, he's angry. Makes sense, but still my lips curl and twitch. I lay on the accent, ridiculously thick.

"Ah am indeed a redneck. Whatever that means. If it means Ah love pickup trucks and *country* music and *lots* of land composed of nothing but *woods* and pasture and none of those mother-*fucking* subdivisions where *you* come from, Ah'm your man. *If* it means Ah grew up on what you might call white-trash food, like scrapple, and pinto beans with chowchow and cornbread, and sausage gravy and buttermilk biscuits, and Vienner sausages, and baloney sandwiches... You eat any of that, pretty boy? Mr. Sophisticate? If not, you will soon, son. Maybe from a goddamn *dawg* deesh, if you ain't more polite. *Sorry* we don't have any arugula and, uh, what? delicate bisques and whatever-the-*fuck*-else is popular these days in urbane food-fashion. *Yes*, I'm a redneck."

Roughly, I massage his buzz-cut, then slap the side of his head. "Cheeky shit. I should take a belt to your shapely butt right now. Or treat you to a sucker-punch. Ah *do* bleeve, to quote my Rebel brothers, that you're *standin'* in need of an *ass*-whippin'."

Rob's visibly cringing beneath my little hillbilly tirade. He bows his head in that defeated, submissive way I'm coming to cherish.

"*Hey*! Uh! *Dude*! Damn, I'm sorry! Don't hit me, okay? I didn't mean...don't be angry, please? I'll eat whatever you wanna feed me; I'm not picky. But... I'm sorry I called you a redneck. Christ, my father was a factory worker before he joined the force, so, so, please, *please*, don't be angry, okay?" Nervously he licks his lips and lifts his head. "May I ask you something?"

"Yes." I manage to keep the snarl out of my tone. Pulling a chair up beside him, I cup his chin in one hand and give him another sip of coffee. "Within reason. Some things you don't want to know. If you knew, well..."

"Yeah. I understand. No, this is...something else. I'm really, really scared, because, well, your friend, he, well, he, uh...finished up inside me. And he didn't use a condom, from what I could tell. So..."

"Ah. Yeah. Condoms are not particularly popular in the rapist community, I fear. You can relax, at least about that." I put down the coffee cup and scoot closer. "Jay and I are monogamous. And we both were tested a few weeks ago. We're fine."

Rob releases a long sigh. "Yeah, I'm clean too. So, if I'm gonna die, that's not the way, huh?"

He's so pitiful I can't resist. Wrapping my arms around him, I pull his head onto my shoulder. "Nope," I say. "Not disease." He tenses up again, then just as quickly relaxes, leaning into me. Outside, a mourning dove starts up its sad cooing.

"I know this sounds crazy, but thanks for being kind to me," Rob says. He gives a low laugh. "Never thought I'd be saying that to a kidnapper." We stay like that for a full minute, his handsome head, like guilt and desire, a weight on my shoulder. I stroke his tattooed back and the tape over his eyes. Then I rise, readjust the afghan around him, give him another sip of coffee, and start frying scrapple.

chapter seven

Rob's ravenous. He gulps down the three slices of scrapple I cut up and feed to him, along with two fried eggs, toast, and a second cup of coffee. Afterwards, he sits quietly in the dark cocoon the blindfold makes of his world while I stack the dishes. Finished, I settle into the chair beside him to finish my coffee.

"Got enough to eat?" I sit back and study him: the beard shadow dusting his cheeks and chin, the tape across his pale chest, his pink nipples, soft cock, and hairy thighs.

"Yes." Rob licks his lips. "It was really good." He hangs his head. "Thank you. C-considering the circumstances, you're being really, uh, considerate."

"How's your butt?" I ask, wiping crumbs off the tabletop.

"Better. This cushion helps."

"I know." I laugh quietly. "The first time Jay fucked me I almost cried. He's pretty damn big."

"He does that to you? He fucks you the way...he fucked me?"

"Yes. He's my lover. It's part of the way we make love."

"He's the Top?"

"Yes."

"Always?"

"Yes. I like it when he fucks me. Love it, actually. I get into this head space where I'm growling and bucking beneath him like some kind of beast. Sometimes I cum without even touching my dick."

"Really? I can't imagine that." Rob shakes his head. "It hurt bad. I thought he was gonna split me in half."

"It doesn't have to hurt. He didn't use lube, and he forced you, so it hurt. He doesn't have to force me. He plays with my nipples—which makes me downright ache to be screwed—and then he takes me hard. It makes me feel...cared for, complete. It makes me feel—I guess this is obvious—full."

Rob cocks his head. "It doesn't make you feel like a woman?"

I guffaw. "A woman? Hell, no! It makes me feel like a man. If it's done right, well, you might learn to enjoy it."

"Doubt it. May I...may I ask you a few other questions?"

"Yes, though I may not answer them."

"Where is he? Your buddy, uh, your lover? Will he be back soon?"

"He's put the fear of God into you, hasn't he? He's at work. I work from home, telecommuting on the computer. I'm your...keeper, so I'll be staying here with you most of the time. Jay will be back this evening."

"He scares me bad, dude. He's pretty brutal."

"Yep. Good reason for you to behave, huh?"

"I guess so." Rob sighs. "How'd you know I'd be jogging that morning, down the Huckleberry Trail? When you two grabbed me?"

"I've been watching you for a long time, Rob. I know where you like to jog and when. I know who your girlfriend is and where she lives. I know where your apartment is. I know how much you like the margaritas and calzones at the Cellar, how much you like to get shit-faced at the Underground Pub and walk home in the rain. Hell, I even know how much you bench-press at the Weight Club. An impressive amount. I loved watching you lift; I loved watching you run through your gymnastic routines. You're really good."

"Shit. How long have you been watching me?

"Months. Your fate—your sojourn here—has been pretty much decided for a good while."

"Oh, God." Rob slumps in the chair. He takes a deep breath, the tight tape creasing his chest. "And there isn't anything I can say to change your mind and let me go? P-please, dude. Don't let him...rape me again. Please? I'm so scared, man. *Please* let me go."

Rob's lips quiver; for a second I'm afraid he's going to start crying again. Then his stubbly jaw firms up. He sits erect, and he continues.

"I don't know who you guys are; I don't know where I am. So if you let me go, I won't be able to tell anyone anything that'd identify you. You seem like a good guy. *Please* don't let him hurt me. I don't deserve any of this. If you don't let me go, I'm afraid he'll really hurt me. Or worse."

My stomach constricts. I rise. "That's enough talk. I'm your captor, not your buddy. I think it's time I took you upstairs and taped your mouth."

"No. No. Please."

"You're not going to fight me, are you?" I grip Rob's arm and pull him to his feet. "Jay's not the only one with a knife. Jay's not the only one who'll punish you if you struggle."

"No," Rob whispers. "No, I won't fight."

We take the stairs slowly, my young captive swaying in his private darkness. In the back bedroom, the usual: application of ball and tape to Rob's mouth, tape to his ankles, chain to his neck. "Take a nap," I say, covering him with blankets. "I'll be just downstairs. I'll be up later to help you piss if you need to. And I'll fetch you some soup come lunchtime. If Jay gives me any grief over these blankets, well, I'll handle him. I won't have you coming down with pneumonia."

I sit in the rocking chair for a while, watching Rob as he shifts about on the bed, trying to get comfortable despite the tape's constrictions. He falls still at last, his breathing grows deep, and now he's snoring softly. From the bedside table, I fetch Jay's knife, a blade I bought him for his last birthday. I unsheathe and stroke it—the black handle, the black steel blade with its thin edges of silver. I test it against my palm. Very sharp. Ready to open a man's body at the slightest provocation. Then I sheathe it and head downstairs to clean up the kitchen.

chapter eight

JAY'S DRUNK AS a lord. I can tell by the way he tosses his coat onto the back of the couch and drops his keys on the kitchen counter.

"It's eight PM. You're two hours late," I complain, ladling chili into bowls.

Jay gives me a quick, hard hug as he passes. He opens the fridge, pulls out a beer bottle, pops it, and takes a long swig. "The boys, they, after work, they took me down to Kasimir's, that bar, y'know, out near the ball park. Just had a few beers and a cigar." He sits heavily in his customary chair, crumbles some Saltines into the chili, adds some Texas Pete hot sauce, and swallows a heaping spoonful. "Damn, good!" Jay looks up at me, blue eyes gleaming. "My favorite." His spoon taps the bowl's edge, an anxious staccato. "Thanks, baby. Best husbear ever!"

There's something different about his behavior this evening. It's worrisome. As shady as some of Jay's work buddies are, and as much meth and other chemical shit that can be found in this little town, I'm always worried that his substance use will get out of hand, especially considering all those prison years he's tried so hard to forget.

"You're drunk," I say. "Are you high too?"

"Hell, no, baby," he says. "Just beer at Kasimir's. Well, and a little of Ben's bong. How's our guest?"

"He's all right. He's asleep upstairs. His asshole's hurting."

"Good!" says Jay, taking a gulp of beer. "Did he give you any trouble?"

"No. The boy's been very obedient."

"Did you fuck him yet?"

"Not yet."

"But y'want to, right?"

"What do you think?"

"I think you're missing one hellava ride."

Jay slams the beer down. It foams over. "Shit!" Giggling, he deep-throats the bottle, takes a big swig, then a second, then a third, finishing it. "Ah! Good stuff! Want one?"

"Might as well." I fetch a brew and ladle out my own meal. I sit across from Jay. For a few minutes we eat in silence.

"Baby, I think I've gotta go to Richmond tomorrow," Jay says. His voice is higher than normal, nervous. "With the guys. Work-related stuff. I think they're gonna meet me down at the mouth of the holler right after noon. Think you can handle the kid for a few days? Just a couple of days."

"Richmond?" I sound irritated, but I guess I don't care how I sound. "All right. I guess. Sure, I can handle him. That's what I'm here for, right?"

"Baby." Jay reaches over and gives my shoulder a gentle punch. "You're here because I love you. And one of the reasons I love you is 'cause you've been so goddamn understanding about, uh, him. Our taped-up little bitch upstairs. My need for reprisal."

"Look, Jay," I say, steeling myself. "About Rob. I covered him with blankets. If he gets sick—that room is so cold—"

To my surprise, Jay shrugs. "Don't matter." He stands up, meal only half-eaten. "Hey, Al, honey, I forgot to pick up some stuff at the store. I'll be back." He plants a sloppy kiss on my forehead, grabs his keys, and disappears out the door. There's the sound of his truck spinning off in the endless rain. Shaking my head, I open another beer, fill another bowl with chili, and head upstairs to give our hostage dinner.

chapter nine

ROB DOESN'T HAVE much to say tonight, and neither do I. He eats his chili, drinks half the beer. He thanks me, submits without a word when I gag him again, rolls onto his side, and lies there, once more a silent sculpture. I bring in a rickety old space heater to warm up this chill tomb of a room, tuck him in, and read in the rocking chair for an hour or two, a strangely squalid novel by William Faulkner called *Sanctuary*. By eleven, Rob's asleep, and Jay hasn't returned. I lock our hostage in for the night, read in my own bed for a while, listen to rain on the tin roof, worry about Jay, and fall asleep.

I wake with a full bladder. Jay's still gone. The clock says two AM. Clambering from bed, I shamble down the hall to the toilet and enjoy a long piss. Returning to bed, I hear a sound. It's whispering, coming from Rob's room. The door's unlocked, open a crack. Inside, the darkness is interrupted by the flicker of candles. The space heater is humming. Silently I push the door open wider.

"Yeah. Yeah. My little bitch. Yeah. My sweet, tight-assed little cum-dump." Jay's standing beside the bed, his back to me. The thick muscles of his back flex in the candlelight; his broad, hairy butt-cheeks contract and relax, contract and relax as he thrusts and sighs.

I step into the room; beneath me a floorboard creaks. Jay turns, sees me, and smiles. Like me, he's unmasked. "Hey, baby," he rasps. "Hey, Al. Come on in."

I obey. I stand at the foot of the bed. Silently I watch.

Rob's bent over the side of the mattress, across a towel-draped pile of pillows, his feet on the floor, his hips in the air, his tape-swathed face buried in the sheets. Though his wrists are still secured behind him, the tape that once wrapped his torso and arms have been removed, lying in sliced strips on the floor. His legs are spread; Jay's fucking him from behind, very slowly, with a tenderness that amazes me. He grips Rob's hips, every now and then adjusting the angle, every now and then bending over to kiss Rob's back, squeeze his taped hands, or ruffle his hair. Even more amazing, they're both weeping. No noise, no sobs, just an occasional sigh and copious tears, flowing beneath Rob's blindfold, adding a glisten to the tape over his mouth, and streaking my partner's dark-stubbled face. "Sweet, sweet. Good little guy," Jay says hoarsely. "Man, I love this. Yeah, that's right. You're learning. Squeeze me...yeah! Right!"

My throat's tight. I pull the rocking chair around to the bed's foot, settle into it, and watch. They weep; Jay pumps in and out; Rob sighs and rocks, entirely acquiescent except for a rare whimper or wince. Now Jay pulls out. He takes the knife from the table.

"Jay?" I say, half-rising. Jay stares at me, his cheeks gleaming wet. His erection bounces; his lips tremble. He wipes his face and smiles. "I won't hurt this boy, Al. Not tonight. I swear. I'm even using lube this time. Okay? Just watch, okay?"

I believe him. He seems half-crazy, probably drunk or drugged or some combination of the two, but I've never seen greater sincerity in his eyes. When I nod, Jay grins, turning back to the bound boy on the bed. I watch as he eases his cock halfway up inside Rob. "All right, bitch?" Jay says. I've never heard "bitch" said with greater affection. Rob lifts his head, grunts, and nods. Jay runs the flat of the knife across Rob's shoulder blades, then taps an ass-cheek with the blade. "Back up onto me, little bitch-boy. Pretty little bitch-boy. Sweet little bitch-boy." Rob does as he's told, cocking his ass and pushing back until Jay's prick is buried to the balls.

"Ahhhhh." Jay recommences his fucking, one hand grasping Rob's lean hip, the other stroking Rob's broad back with the side of the knife. He's thrusting very slowly, very deeply, pulling almost all the way out, working Rob's hole with his fat cockhead before sliding in again. If it weren't for the fact that Rob's our prisoner, and, despite his complete compliance, tearful and unwilling, I'd think that they were making love. Far from the whimpers and struggles of last night, Rob seems to have surrendered to his rapist and to his fate utterly.

"I'm going to cut you now, boy," Jay whispers, wiping his wet eyes with the back of his hand. "Remember what I said before, okay? Just a scratch, okay? As long as you don't fight me, just a scratch. Okay? I swear."

Jay pulls out, slaps Rob's butt-cheeks with the side of his dick, rubs his cockhead up and down Rob's ass-crack, then pushes up inside him again, eliciting from Rob a moan of what could be pain or could be pleasure. "If you fight me, I'll sink this blade in your side, and this ride'll be over. Over for good. Okay? Going to be a good little bitch? My little bitch?"

To my surprise, Rob grunts and nods. "Uh huh! Uh huh! Ya!" I suppose if I were totally at a man's mercy, and he gave me such a choice, I'd do the same.

"Keep real still." Jay gives our captive's butt a few short cock-prods before pushing in to the hilt. He pats a butt-cheek and lifts the knife.

I think about stopping him. I should stop him. But it's all too fucking beautiful. Instead I stand; I stroke Rob's head, then steady him with a hand pressed upon his neck.

"Ready?" says Jay.

"Mm mm," Rob mumbles before drawing a deep breath.

Jay presses down, running the tip of the knife from the base of Rob's neck down his spine, over the swirling flames of ink, finishing just above his prick-impaled ass-cheeks. It is indeed just a scratch, not even a deep one, but the knife is very sharp. In its wake, a thin line of blood wells up.

"Now the crossbeam." Jay begins on Rob's left shoulder blade, drawing the knife-point down across the valley of the backbone, where vertical and horizontal axes meet, and finishing on the swell of Rob's right shoulder blade. More blood wells in that fine, fine furrow.

Throughout the process, our victim—the boy could be a sacrifice bleeding on some pagan altar—has kept perfectly still, and silent save for shallow breaths. Jay smiles at me; I smile back, my fascinated, perverse heart pounding, my mouth dry. "Fucking lovely," he says. "Might leave a scar; might not. Don't matter. You're mine now. You're mine." Bending, he laps at Rob's bloody back. He lifts his head, and, with smeared and smiling lips, he kisses me. Sweet and salt and steel on my tongue.

"Not done yet. Right, Rob?"

"Umm um." Beneath my grip, Rob shakes his head. He's so submissive he seems hypnotized or drugged.

As if reading my mind, Jay says, "Yeah, I gave him just a tetch of something. A relaxant Ben sold me. Thought that might loosen him up some. It worked. Ain't he all limber, laid-back, and easy?" Jay pulls his cock out and pushes aside the heap of pillows. "Roll him over, Al. Center him on the towel."

Entranced, I obey. Jay grips Rob's hips, pulls him closer, hoists his legs over his shoulders, bends the boy double, and slides inside him with one thrust. A tiny groan escapes Rob; otherwise, he stays quiet. Jay rides him for a full minute, pumping gently, before coming to rest deep inside.

"Hold him down," Jay says. He bends over, kisses Rob's heaving chest, and lifts the knife again.

I grip Rob's shoulders, gazing down at the high forehead, the handsome face concealed by feet of tear-shiny silver-gray.

"Ready for the second cross?"

Rob nods, taking another deep breath. Jay cuts him, a fine furrow from the top of his breastbone down between his pecs, through his navel, to the top of his pubic bush. Next, the horizontal, a few millimeters above his nipples, from the far edge of Rob's firm right pec-mound across his chest to the far edge of the left. The blood flows more freely this time. It makes a tiny pool in the cleft between Rob's pecs and trickles down his sides onto the towel.

Jay licks the knife-tip clean, places it on the bed at a safe distance, and starts thrusting into Rob's ass again. "Drink?" Jay says.

My mouth is on the wounded boy's chest before I know what I'm doing. I lick like a starving cat, lapping up the little pool, rubbing my beard over the blood till its seeping has stopped and my face is wet. Jay chuckles. We bend together over Rob and kiss, mouths shoved together, tongues frantic. We're still kissing when Jay gasps, bucks into Rob's ass, and climaxes with a low growl.

chapter ten

HYDROGEN PEROXIDE AND cotton balls. "That'll do," Jay says. "No bandages. No need. I want to see his wounds."

We're stretched out on the bed, Rob between us. I swab the cuts on his back first; Rob flinches a few times, head lolling dazedly. Gently I roll him over and do the same to his chest; he jolts, then, panting, falls still. Jay's pulled our hostage's head onto his shoulder and wrapped a big arm around him, whispering to him as I play nurse. "You're all right, aren't you, boy? I didn't hurt you too bad, now did I? Big strong boy, muscles everywhere...you did good, kid. Real good. Our brave little drugged-out boy. Took it. Tough boy took it. All marked up. Pretty. Our little Christ, huh, Al? Our own little cut-up Christ. Our sweet cum-dump, our sweet butt-bitch."

They're sleeping now, on their sides, Rob's fetal curl tucked into Jay's hairy arms. If it weren't for the remaining bonds, they could be lovers on some idyllic honeymoon. I sit in the rocking chair and listen to their deep breaths, mingling with the occasional snort or snore and the continuous whirring of the heater. I rock, the bloody towel in my lap. The candles burn down and, one by one, burn out. When the last one dies, I lift the towel to my lips, smell and taste the remnants of Rob's blood, then leave my men to sleep. I read in the front bedroom for a while, more sordid Faulkner, before turning off the light. I toss and turn for another hour, listening to the wind gust and the old house creak, before finally drifting off.

chapter eleven

JAY SNAPS THE phone shut. "Fuck! They're coming up the holler! They'll be here any minute. Get your ass upstairs! You got to keep that boy quiet!"

I just about drop the dish I'm drying. "Wouldn't it be better to move him to the basement? That room without windows? Or drug him?"

"Ain't time, goddamn it! Git! They say they want some beers before we leave. My knife's up there if he gives you any fight. Go on now!"

I toss the dishrag on the counter and dash up the stairwell. Unlatching the padlock, I slip inside the back bedroom and lock the door behind me. "It's me," I say to the figure huddled on the mattress.

Rob's in his usual fetal position. I pull back the blankets and take a couple of seconds to look him over, making sure that his bonds are still snugly in place. This morning, at Jay's insistence, I added more tape to the boy's wrists and taped up his torso, arms, and ankles again. He's got a strong odor, due to his rigorous but futile struggles and days denied a shower. It's so cold in here—the shitty-cheap space heater stopped working in the middle of the night—that goose pimples cover his knife-scored chest and breath drifts from his nostrils in wisps of fog. There's Jay's hunting knife atop the bedside table. I pick it up before sitting beside our shivering hostage.

"Look, kid, we're about to get unexpected visitors, so you need to keep very quiet."

We chose this old house for its isolation: set deep in spruce woods, way up a mountain cove at the head of a holler. No one other than Jay and I have been near here since Rob's abduction—we pick up our mail in town. So this is the first chance that Rob's had to alert the outside world to his captivity.

Compliant as he was last night, still he's a cop's son, brought up to be a scrapper. Six feet tall, all muscle, he's in perfect shape. Jay's cut him and raped him; sooner or later, hot and helpless as Rob is, as white, curved and superlative as is his ass, I might slough off what're left of my morals and do the same. The boy's terrified and would, given the chance, no doubt do just about anything to escape. All these factors add up to one thing: sudden, desperate defiance.

Rob starts to shout. His gag may be multilayered and extensive, but the noise fills the room the way a bad-moonshine hangover can fill the skull. His voice starts deep, a baritone roar, like storm wind in evergreens, then climbs higher, a shrill tenor, a frantic bawling for help.

I should have known better. Wrong move. Stupid, stupid.

"Ohhh, fuck!" I sigh. The noise batters me, auditory hailstones. It makes my head throb with guilt and my belly tar up with fear.

Jay's told me a lot about prison. Our boy's just made all this a little easier and me a little less conflicted. I need to get tough now, or Jay and I are going to be arrested for kidnapping.

Time to put kindness away. I throw myself on top of Rob, roll him onto his side, slam my hand over his mouth, and press the side of the knife to his forehead.

"And I thought you and I had come to an understanding after all our talk. You know what this is, don't you, son?"

Rob strains against me and keeps screaming.

I snicker. "Ah, you know I'm the soft-hearted one, huh? 'Considerate,' you said. You think? You sure? I got news for you. I got something in common with Jay: disobedience makes me mean."

I shove him over onto his belly and fling myself on top. The air's slammed out of him; his yelling's cut short. Rob's very strong, but not as strong as well applied, thickly applied duct tape, and, besides, I have a good fifty pounds on him. Like Jay, I'm burly with muscle and fast-food fat. If any man can subdue a boy this fit, I can.

Rob gasps beneath my weight, trying to catch his breath so he can start screaming again. "Oh, no, you don't." I clamp my hand more tightly over his taped mouth and press the knife against his windpipe. "Listen to me. Give me one minute, and then, if you want, you can start shouting for help again."

Rob struggles and bucks, but, between the tight bonds and my heft, it's a pointless attempt.

"Give me a minute, or I'll cut your throat right now."

He nods weakly against my grip and stops squirming.

"Okay, look, kid, I've tried to be good to you despite the circumstances. You're right: I have a soft heart. You break my heart, actually. Hell, I'm a little in love with you. I've wanted you, and now I have you. I intend to keep you. And I'm not going to prison. I've heard about prison. So," I say, squeezing his stubbly jaw, "you have several choices. I can put this pillow over your face and suffocate you. I can cut your throat. Or you can shut up now and just let me snuggle with you, let me warm you up some until our visitors leave. What do you say?"

Rob's straining lessens; drool wells around the tape, wetting my hand.

"Going to behave?"

He nods. With a deep shudder, he goes limp.

"Good boy," I say, rolling us back onto our sides so that he can breathe easier. Submissive he appears to be, but I keep my hand over his mouth and the blade against his throat anyway. "Let's just lie here for a while. Jay's leaving with them on a three-day business trip, so I plan to make you as comfortable as possible while he's gone. Gonna wrap you in warm blankets, cook you some good meals. Sound nice?"

"Uh huh," Rob grunts. Downstairs a door opens; male voices filter up through the floor. They're here. I pull my silent captive closer. My cock's a hard ache in my jeans.

chapter twelve

"HE DESERVES IT, so stop arguing," Jay whispers. "When I get back, I wanna see that little bastard's back and butt bruised up bad. If y'need to go to the store for anything, hogtie him and leave him in the basement. Or drug the fucker. That stuff we used to knock him out is in the bathroom."

The guys downstairs have spent nearly an hour drinking. Now they're all heading out, driving to Richmond. Jay's up here giving me last-minute orders, his travel bag at his feet. Rob lies on the bed, back to us but no doubt taking in every word.

"Bye, baby," Jay says, giving me a hurried but passionate kiss. "I'll miss you."

I gaze into his icy blue eyes and rub the black stubble on his chin. "I'll miss you too. Don't worry; I'll take good care of our friend here. He isn't going anywhere." I've risked so much for Jay. Sometimes I regret it; mostly I don't. I don't know how I'd live without him.

"Get yourself some of this while I'm gone," Jay says. He gropes Rob's bare rear; Rob tenses and grunts. "One of the best rides I've ever had. Other than you," he adds, squeezing my denimed butt before lifting his travel bag and heading out the door.

I lock the door behind him. His heavy tread descends the stairs. The front door slams; voices commingle on the porch. Then engines start up, cars retreat down the holler, and we're left in chilly silence.

"You heard what he said," I sigh. With a finger, I trace the black flames inked into Rob's muscled back. "You really should never have started that stupid shouting. I told you you'd be punished if you disobeyed us."

I unlock Rob's neck chain; with the knife, I cut his feet free. "Up," I say, helping him sit. When he tries to stand, he can't, slumping back onto the mattress. His legs have been bound so long I guess they're sore.

"Oh hell. Buck up, boy. You're too big to carry. If you can't walk, I'll have to drag you. Come on; let's get this over with."

I grip my prisoner by the shoulders; he takes a deep breath and stands. He sways, legs trembling. "Lean on me," I say. He does. Slowly we make our way across the room, down the hall, down the stairs, across the kitchen, and down rickety steps into the basement.

FOR A GOOD while, his wincing makes me wince, his writhing makes me hurt, his gagged screams wound me. But I guess I've been with Jay long enough to have learned cruelty, so eventually I begin to grow aroused and enjoy myself, to savor the way such a beautiful body jolts and shakes beneath my blows. It's thrilling, to have such power, to make a boy so desirable feel so deeply.

Rob's back is to me, his legs spread, his torso pressed against a basement post. I've secured him to it with rope, several yards at the neck, more at the waist. I don't have access to his lower back, since his crossed wrists are taped together there, so I focus on his blade-etched upper back and shoulders. I'm using my doubled-over leather belt. I beat him as Jay had demanded, till red welts cover his inked muscles and some of the cuts made last night begin to bleed again. I keep beating him even after his initial stoic grunts have turned to stifled sobbing and he's begging me to stop.

Second phase. I unrope him from the post. He slumps onto his knees, whimpering and shaking. I drag him over to the chair, sit on it, and haul him onto my lap, across my sadism-stiff hard-on. I run the belt over his butt; I run my fingers over his wet beard. "Ready?"

He shakes his head violently.

"Too bad. Get through this, don't struggle, just take it, and I'll make the time Jay's gone downright luxurious for you, okay?"

Long hesitation, then a feeble nod. I rest my forearm across his back, hold him down, and begin belting his lovely ass.

chapter thirteen

"WHY, HONEY!" SAYS the clerk in the music department. "You wouldn't believe it! Steve Martin—you know, the comedian?—who'd ever have thought he could make good bluegrass? But this CD is great! And this one too, by Alison Krauss!"

We Southerners make a social interaction out of everything, which means friendliness abounds but everything takes twice the amount of time it should. I came to Magic Mart to find a new space heater, was tempted by a display of new country music CDs, and now am listening to this pleasant-looking middle-aged woman go on about bluegrass. What would she say if she knew I had a naked hostage bound and gagged in my basement? I imagine the expression on her face and almost laugh out loud.

Instead, I say, "Thanks very much, ma'am. I much appreciate the suggestions; I'll keep all that in mind." Mannerliness and casual chat are second-nature to me, just like other folks from southwest Virginia. "Right now, though, could I buy this Billy Currington CD? And in what department would I find space heaters?"

"Why, yes, certainly," she says, ringing up the CD. "Billy Currington, he's so handsome. And what a voice! I love that song he does about turnip greens. Well, anyway, honey, if you go down that aisle there, you'll find them heaters near the back. I got one of them rotating ones back at home, and it works real well."

What does she see as she smiles at me and bags my purchase? Nothing uncommon, I suspect. A thick-set, muscular guy in his early forties, with a black beard graying at the edges, hazel eyes, a STARS AND BARS FOREVER baseball cap, shaggy hair, dirty jeans, muddy work boots, and a heavy Carhartt jacket. A burly redneck, in other words, just like so many local guys, though shyer, more soft-spoken than most. I grew up a couple of counties over, absorbing the same form of blue-collar manliness as my brothers and buddies. I'm just like them, to some extent. But, well, okay, I'm also wildly different. My submissive ardor for Jay and my tender but raging lust for Rob certainly prove that.

My thoughts stray as I wander the aisles of Magic Mart, tracking down the heater required to keep my captive warm: how much I'm a part of here, of home, and how much I'm not. I guess, even before this foray into kidnapping, I've been more sharply aware than most hill-guys of the sometimes dramatic contrasts between appearance and reality. Growing up in a little mountain town trying to hide my desires for men, I learned early: be manly or be mocked, be tough or be humiliated. Later, in college, I found out how surprised straight people were when I told them I was gay—"You're too masculine, too country to be queer!" and how surprised gay guys were to know that someone so big and butch—scruffy and laconic as any redneck—was an eager bottom, with a crazy hunger to get it up the ass. Yeah, I screwed a few younger, smaller guys, even learned to pleasure a guy's hole, but for the most part I just wanted a big, hairy guy on top of me, hammering away. I was well built and good-looking enough to get sex often, but I was too unsophisticated to keep anyone for long. They all wanted someone slick, urbane, polished. It wasn't till I met Jay—as rough and rural as I, though lacking my college degree—that I found someone who was willing to stick around, to make me his partner and full-time bottom. Which is why, I suppose, I've risked so much to keep him.

So much for my lonely history. Here are the heaters. This one's Honeywell. Nice brand name. Ought to keep our honey well-warmed, keep our honey-well cozy, keep the goose pimples off our honey-boy's big chest and curvy ass. God, that ass. The brown hair so soft and thick between those white, hard cheeks. I guess I'm no longer just Jay's bottom, am I? Right now I'm in automatic-consumer-mode, chatting with yet another friendly clerk as I buy the heater, my surface all pleasantry, but inside my head's a whirlpool. I keep thinking about leaving Rob on the hard floor of the basement, how his naked body strained against his new bonds and his painful new position, how he whimpered against his gag—pathetic little mews—when, ascending the stairs, I left him. God, the boy's as beautiful as they come, all cut-up and white, trussed, unbathed, and trembling. I want to drive straight home, take him right there on the cold concrete, eat and slap and spear his ass, use him hard, despite his pain and his fear, pump a big load up his burning hole.

Fuck, I'm hard in my jeans. Glad this winter jacket is long enough to hide the bulge. After watching Jay with Rob last night, how tenderly, almost reverentially he fucked him and cut him, and after all I've felt and continue to feel for our captive—well, now that the boy, however unwillingly, is part of our household, I think Jay and I are as hot for Rob as we are for one another, if not more so. Inevitable, I guess, after our years of monogamy. Most of the long-term male couples I've gotten to know don't even have sex any longer, or are in open relationships. Jay and me, well, I still love it when he pounds me, though such well-lubed scenes are rarer than they used to be.

Ah, fuck it. I've got lots of buying yet to do before I get home to Rob's taped-tight warmth. Liquor store for George Dickel. All those references to whiskey sours in Faulkner's novel have made me crave them. Another chatty clerk, another spasm of "if they only knew." Then Food City for groceries—cheeses, eggs, cornmeal, buttermilk, more scrapple, Jimmy Dean sausage, coffee, beef, potatoes, cabbage, chicken, beer, wine, even the sweet splurge of a cake. Always wise to keep the pantry well stocked this time of year in case a big snow seals us up the holler for a few days. There's the cute bag-boy, with his sharp nose, bushy uni-brow, and patchy beard; here's the arrogant butcher-boy with the long sideburns and the broad, plump ass I'd like to belt hard before I rode him. And hot, hot Tim McGraw on the cover of *Country Weekly*. Bet he'd look mighty fine tied belly-down on the bed with a pair of my rank underwear stuffed in his mouth.

Funny how dominant my fantasies are becoming. Used to be, before I met Jay, I wanted to grab my ankles for every hot country boy I passed, but now, suddenly, I'm more in the mood to ram than be rammed. I've always been an incorrigible horn-dog, much to Jay's delight, but knowing that Rob's back home, waiting for me, no doubt fighting his bonds in the basement dark, just makes my libido burn a hundred times hotter.

The winter sky's a flat, curdled gray, like iced-over brook water, by the time I finish shopping at Food City. Cold rain recommences as I load up the truck. One last stop at Poor Boys Produce—the stern-voiced woman with the big hair recommends the fresh fried pies, so I pick up a few, along with some yellow-eye beans, sorghum, sourdough bread, and fatback—then I'm heading through town, on the way home to Rob.

Talk about post-industrial. I pass one abandoned storefront after another, and, in the center of town, the huge furniture factories, abandoned for years now, with their crumbled walls of brick, aerial tubes like octopus tentacles, empty sheds, unlit or broken windows, rail tracks that go nowhere. So many folks in this county are unemployed and dirt-poor. I'm lucky to have my online job; Jay's lucky to have his sawmill position. And now we have another mouth to feed. Two Daddies and a reluctant son.

Sleet's returned, pinging off the windshield. I turn off the paved highway onto the dirt road up the holler, shifting into four-wheel-drive as I do. It's muddy, bumpy, a hard climb even in a 4x4 truck. Halfway up the mile-long hill, the gray limbs of oak and tulip tree turn to evergreens, the light grows less beneath the boughs of spruce. I bounce into the little clearing before the house. The building's dirty white, in bad need of a paint job, two-storied, with a double porch and a sloping tin roof green with age.

And in the concrete and cinderblock space underneath the house, Rob lies, cold and suffering, his ears straining for my arrival. His life is entirely in my hands. If for some reason I were not to return, if Jay were not to return, the boy could scream and scream for days, piss and shit himself, fight his bonds till he bled, thrash around on the floor and sob, and no one would ever hear him. He'd die slowly, of thirst and hunger. The next renters of the house would find the corpse, the skeleton his young life would leave behind, the only evidence that he existed, that Rob Drake once was fit and strong and handsome.

Parking in back, I carry the bags through the screened-in back porch and into the kitchen. Beneath my weight the wood floor groans. Rob can hear it, I know; somehow I can see him, lying there inside the earth, bent double in the dark. He gives a little sob of relief, knowing that his savior has returned, to feed him, to comfort him, to hold him close.

chapter fourteen

ROB'S WHERE I left him, on a blanket on the basement floor, more powerless than ever. He's hogtied on his side, torso and arms taped as before, taped wrists rope-cinched tightly behind his back to roped ankles. His head's resting in a wet patch of drool. He's dislodged his gag somewhat. The tape no longer covers his mouth but threads between his lips. No matter; the ball's still held in place.

"You all right?" I say, kneeling beside him. Even in this dim light, I can see his goose-pimpled shivers. "You're freezing, aren't you?"

Rob groans and nods.

"Sorry about that. I bought you a new space heater." When I stroke his brow, I find it moist. When I check his bonds, I find his roped ankles red-raw.

"Sweaty and chafed? Been trying to get loose, huh? Be honest; I won't beat you again today."

Rob gives a frustrated pant, grits his teeth around the tape, and nods.

"Yeah, I guess I'd do the same. Worked that gag loose some too, I see. Been shouting for help?"

Rob gives a deep sigh.

I chuckle. "No one's gonna hear you, kid. That's why I left you down here. You're underground. No windows in this room." The boy smells sweet, not unwashed, thanks to the lotion I rubbed over his back, torso, and ass after the beating. "Got all the groceries. Some nice Shiraz too. You ready for less constrictive restraint? I'll bet that ball's hurting your jaw by now."

Rob nods vehemently. When I stroke the welts ridging his buttocks, he jumps beneath my touch and gives a hoarse groan. The formerly white curves of his ass are entirely purple and black.

"Damn, you're *really* bruised up. Didn't wet the floor, I see. Good boy. Need to piss?"

Another desperate nod. I unknot the hogtie and help him to his feet. "Ready to go upstairs? I'll set you up in front of the fireplace and break open a bottle of red. You like Swiss steak and mashed potatoes?"

He sways against me. "Mm hm." I wipe slobber from his chin, wrap an arm around him, and assist him up the steps.

chapter fifteen

ROB LOOKS ALMOST content on the couch, nestled beneath an afghan. I guess when you've been stuck in hell, some time in purgatory is damned sweet.

My prisoner gave me not the slightest struggle as I rearranged his restraints, probably because I promised to make his bondage less painful. I've cuffed his wrists before him, rope-tethered the cuffs to the short chain connecting his manacled ankles, and taped his arms and elbows to his torso and waist. He is, in other words, still secured but now fairly comfy. The effect's much like that of hunched and shackled prisoners in maximum-security prisons or on death row. I've loosely knotted a bandana around his neck, ready to use when the time comes to gag him again.

"Here," I say, lifting the nearly empty wineglass to his mouth. There's tape adhesive clotting his beard, but I leave it there. I like the look of it. Rob takes a long slurp, licks his lips, and sighs his thanks. I readjust the blanket about him and add a log to the fire before heading into the kitchen to check on the potatoes and open another bottle of Shiraz.

More hard rain tonight. The usual cove-fog swathes the house; the tin roof drums with storm. I drain the potatoes, mash them with butter and cream, and spoon them into a covered dish to microwave later. Steak's not yet sufficiently tender, so I add some canned mushrooms and leave it to bake longer.

My cell-phone buzzes: it's Jay. "Hey, Shweet Hole," he slurs, one of his many vulgar love-names for me.

"You sound very drunk," I say, shaking my head. "What you swilling this time?"

"Ohhh, Franklin County moonshine! Want me to bring some home? It's fine stuff. Smooth, smooth."

"Absolutely! You know I love it. I—"

"Look, baby, I can't talk long. Just wanted you to know we got here safe. Ray almost hit some twat of a bicyclist here in town. Guess he had one too many beers at our place. Did you beat that cunt? Drake? Is he black and blue?"

"Yeah, I beat him like you told me to."

"And did you enjoy it?"

"Yeah. I guess I did. Got me hard."

Jay snickers. "Hope for you yet. Don't coddle the bastard. And, hey, watch out, 'cause there's a nasty ice storm heading in from the west. Should hit you first. Might mean I don't get home for a day or so longer, if it's bad enough to fuck up the roads."

Male voices in the background. Laughter. "Hey, okay, I got to go. Ben and Andy need me. Miss you, honey. I'll see you probably day after tomorrow." Before I can respond, Jay ends the call.

Ray. Andy. Ben. I've met all his sawmill friends. Shiftless drunks. Irresponsible. Nasty little boys in men's bodies. Too often lately, Jay's come home very late and very drunk, his dinner cold. We argue; he apologizes; he gets sad-eyed and pathetic, begs me not to leave him, then takes me upstairs, ties me to the bed, claps his hand over my mouth, and ass-fucks me so hard I'm wet-eyed and begging him for more. Damned effective way to make me forgive all his shortcomings.

Well, I forgive. That doesn't mean I stop worrying, especially about what he plans to do with Rob. When I return to the den, our hostage is stretched out on the couch, snoring softly. When I ruffle his hair, he jolts awake.

"Al?" he says, sitting up, fear in his voice.

"Who else?" I slip onto the couch, rest his head in my lap, and pull the afghan over his bare shoulders. "You fell asleep. I guess you ought to be exhausted after all you've been through. How're your cuffs? Are you more comfortable bound like this?"

"*God*, yes. Much better. My shoulders and arms were killing me before."

"You warm enough? Like the fire?"

"Oh, yeah. It feels good. I'm a little buzzed. I'm hurting pretty bad, but the wine helps. Why did you have to beat me?"

I sigh, rubbing the band of duct-tape over his eyes. "I'm not as cruel as Jay, but I won't tolerate resistance any more than he would. You need to obey us. Or else. You try to escape, and I'll whip you till there's nothing left of that fine physique but a blubbering ball of agony."

"Please don't say things like that. I'm already scared shitless. I'll obey you, I swear. Just please don't beat me again."

I take a sip of wine, then angle his head so he can take another big slurp. I want this boy drunk tonight.

"Well, if you do what I say, I promise to make you feel as good as possible."

"Are you all ever gonna let me go?"

"As delicious as you're looking right now, my inclination is to keep you captive forever. I don't know, kid. Once we pick up the ransom, maybe."

"Are you gonna...you gonna kill me? Once you get the money?"

"Only if you try to get loose." That's a lie. I still don't know whether Jay will decide to off him or whether I'll let Jay do that if the time comes. "Like I said before, if you work that blindfold off and see our faces, you're a dead man. So keep the tape on, okay?"

"Okay. I promise." Rob snuggles into the afghan and exhales. "Look, my asshole still hurts, though last night wasn't half as bad as the first time. I'm almost glad he drugged me. It made it all easier to take. But still, uh, are you...tonight, are you going to fuck me too? Please don't."

"I certainly want to...to take you that way. Eventually. Not yet. I can't help but want to make love to you, Rob. You're beautiful."

"How can you make love to me if I'm not gay, dude? It isn't lovemaking if you do it against a guy's will."

"You like your cock sucked?"

"Yeah," Rob mutters. "Sure. I'm like most guys; I love a good blow job. Long as Sarah's doing it."

"Sarah isn't here. I am." I caress his torso with a forefinger. "Behave, okay? I'm going to touch you for a while."

Rob bites his lower lip and nods. I stroke a nipple. Immediately, it hardens beneath my fingers.

"Does that feel good?"

"It doesn't feel bad." Rob gives a faint smile.

I flick the tit, tug at the fine hair circling it, and pinch it tenderly. "Do the cuts Jay made hurt you?"

"No. He kept his word: they're just scratches. They stung a little at first, when he cut me and for a while after, but now I can't feel them at all."

"You were very brave to endure that, to keep so quiet and still."

"Uh, dude, what choice did I have? I was drugged half out of my mind. Your buddy told me he was going to do it—was going to fuck me and cut me—no matter what. Told me if I didn't be strong I'd suffer worse." Rob shrugs. "Shit, sure I'm traumatized, but, after the several times my dad's been shot in the line of duty, the least I can do is take a few scratches. Hell, really, what's a sore asshole and some cuts to a bullet wound? Dad taught me that manhood's about being stoic. Guess it's just my turn to bleed, huh? To suffer? Lord knows my life's been pretty easy and sheltered. At least up to the other morning, when we, uh, met. On the jogging trail."

I kiss his forehead. I sigh.

Rob licks his lips. "He drank my blood, didn't he?"

"Yes."

"And you did too?"

"Yes." I run a finger over his upper lip, then over the brown stubble coating his chin.

"Wow," he whispers, shaking his blind head. "Why?"

"I can't speak for him. I did it to be closer to you. To have some of you inside of me." I run a finger along the vertical arm of his torso-cross, then along the horizontal. "This doesn't hurt?"

"No. Thanks for putting lotion on me this morning, dude. It eased what pain there was. The belting hurt a hell of a lot worse than the cutting, by the way."

"Sorry about that. It was necessary." I press my palm against his breast and knead lightly. "You have a magnificent chest. Just fucking amazing pecs. How does that feel?"

"Uh, good." Tensing, Rob takes a sharp intake of breath. "Yeah. Yeah, it does."

I move my attentions to the other nipple-nub, circling it with a finger before squeezing it lightly. "Relax, kid. I'm not going to hurt you. I want to make you feel good. I want you to get hard now, okay? If you need to think about your girlfriend, do it. Just get hard for me."

"I don't think—"

"Bullshit. You're twenty-two. When I was your age, I had an erection three-fourths of the time."

"Yeah, but I'm really scared. Okay. I'll try," Rob whispers. He's begun trembling. "Just...p-please don't hurt me if I can't. Don't get angry, okay? Don't beat me again."

"I promise." Slipping off the couch, I fall to my knees beside him and pull the afghan off him. He lies back, a study in white skin, lean muscle, and silver-gray tape, his trembling become a visible shudder. "I want to suck your tits, Rob. Okay if I suck your tits?"

Rob gulps. "Y-yeah."

Bending, I take his left nipple in my mouth and grip his limp penis in my fist.

"God, you taste good," I growl. "Tender, salty..." Years of being Jay's lover have given me a strong preference for rough lovemaking, both in the giving and the taking, but this boy's so young, frightened, and damaged, and not exactly eager, so I do my best to be gentle, despite this urge to chew his flesh till he bleeds again.

For long, rapturous minutes, I suck and nibble his chest; I tug his balls and work his cock. Ever so slowly his shaft hardens inside my expert stroking. He emits tiny sighs; his cuffed hands quake; he allows himself a tentative thrust into my hand.

"You fucking Sarah?" I whisper, leaving his chest to lick his chin.

"Yeah, yeah, I am," Rob murmurs. "That's right."

I study his strong jaw, stubbly beard, set lips. "God, you're handsome."

"Even with tape on my face?" Rob snorts, mustering a weak grin.

"God, yes. Kiss me," I say, brushing my beard against his.

"Uhm. I—"

My mouth falls on his. I lick his closed lips. "I said kiss me. Open up now. Do what you're told."

More shudders course through his body. He parts his lips; I push my tongue inside. He lies there, acquiescent, as I explore his wine-savory mouth. Inside my fist, he's half-hard now, a long lean length to match his long, lean frame. I've started a steady rhythm, and now, to my delight—thank God for overripe youth and its wild hormones—he starts earnestly humping my hand.

If there's one thing a man my age knows—twenty years older than Rob, I guess I am—it's the advantages of delaying rapture. I cease my passionate ministrations and stand. Triumph swells my chest. "That meat should be ready by now. Be right back." I leave my captive with moistened lips, stiff nipples, and an unwilling hard-on.

chapter sixteen

WE SIT SIDE by side on the couch. I feed Rob, forkfuls of steak I've cut for him, spoonfuls of mashed potatoes topped with gravy, then store-bought German chocolate cake, sticky chunks I feed him with my fingers. By the time we're done, his mouth and chin are a smeary mess. I lick him clean, a lengthy process that actually inspires in him a boyish giggle. If he's disgusted by my touch, he's damned good at hiding it. But I guess I would be too, if I were in his position.

I straighten up the kitchen, pour us a glass of Scotch to share, and arrange us in our previous position, with Rob stretched out beneath the blanket, his head in my lap. For a while we're silent, listening to the crackle of fire, the ticking of sleet.

"Famous Grouse," I say, holding the glass to Rob's lips. "Like it?"

"Good stuff," he says. "I'm really drunk now. Thanks for the great meal. You Southerners can really cook."

"How do you know I'm a Southerner?" I say, suddenly wary.

"How do I know? Please! Ah, your accent, man! Your vowels. That's part of the reason I asked if you were a redneck before, and, uh, again I apologize for that. You sound like a cross between educated and real country. I know a lot about you, dude. Don't want to fuck up my chances for survival, but it's true. May I have another sip?"

I lift the glass; he slurps.

"What else do you know?"

"Well. You smell like my father. Guess that's Old Spice. You're way bigger'n me. Thick arms. You must be real strong, to be able to move me around the way you do. You have kind of a beer-gut. You have a beard; sometimes you wear a mask. You sound like you're in your late thirties, early forties. You have a...you're hung, 'cause I've felt it against me."

Go on," I say, staring into the fading fire.

"Uh, we're somewhere out in the country, 'cause there are no city sounds around. I can't hear anything but rain and wind and crows, and sometimes a train a long ways away. And, uh, one of your vehicles sure needs a new muffler."

I chuckle. "Correct. That's what the ransom's for. A new muffler. Continue, detective."

"Well, as you said, you're kind of infatuated with me, or at least the way I look, and you're, uh, lusty, so you really want to, to t-take me hard, but you're basically a kind guy, you're doing your damnedest to treat me with compassion, even though, since you got me so helpless, you could do any damn thing you wanted with me and to me...so I guess all this is really hard for you. And you let that other guy, the mean one, Jay, you let him boss you around. He brings out your cruel side. None of this would have happened if it hadn't been for him."

"Wow. Sherlock Holmes, huh? You're not only sexy, you're smart."

"Hey, don't sound so surprised. I was studying—"

"Criminal investigations. I know. I know more about you than you know about me." I finish the Scotch, stand up, and close up the fireplace. "Time for bed."

chapter seventeen

LIFTING ROB TO his feet, I escort his shackled shuffle upstairs. I help him piss before doing the same. In the hallway, I pause, grasping his cuffed hands.

"You have a choice. You can spend the night in that back bedroom where we've been keeping you. I'll turn on the new space heater and cover you with blankets so you'll be warm enough. Or you can sleep in my bedroom."

Rob hesitates for only a moment. "I, uh, don't leave me alone, okay?" he says, voice catching. "I'd rather sleep in your room."

I don't know whether he's trying to ingratiate himself or whether he's simply desperate for any companionship in such dangerous extremity, but I don't care. I grip his elbow. "All right, kid. Come with me." Sleet grows louder against the tin roof as I lead my blinded captive down the hallway and into the bedroom Jay and I share.

"Here we go," I say, helping Rob sit on the edge of the bed. "We have a gas fire in here," I say, turning it on. "It'll keep us nice and snug tonight."

"So you all sleep in this warm room while I shiver in that icebox you keep me in? Pretty cruel, dude."

"Meant to be cruel." I pull the drapes aside and look outside. The fog's so thick I can't see the trees surrounding the house. Tiny flecks of ice bounce off the pane. "You're not exactly our dinner guest, you know."

"Yeah. Well, let's just say I'm glad to be in here tonight." Rob hangs his head and clasps his cuffed hands in his lap. "Oooff! I'm still really drunk." He takes a deep breath, big chest swelling against the strips of tape. He's a picture of pathos. Damned gorgeous.

I pull off my sweatshirt and undershirt. "Look, kid, I know you said you didn't want to be left alone, but I sleep naked. If that scares you, I could make a little bed for you on the floor if you'd like."

Rob lifts his head, blindfolded eyes directed toward my voice. "No," he says firmly. "I want to sleep with you. I suspect you might, uh, get frisky again, but I don't think you're going to hurt me. I'd just be grateful for the company and the body heat. I'm tired of lying in that room in the silence and the cold wondering how much longer I have to live."

How much longer does he have to live? I wish I knew the answer to that.

"Plus, look, you told me you'd make me comfortable. I really don't want to sleep on the floor. I'm sore enough from hours on that basement concrete." He gives me a bleak grin.

"Okay, kid." I unlace my work boots and kick them off; I slip off my jeans and boxer briefs. The chill washes over me. "Let's get you situated. First, let's get these foot-shackles off. I can tell they're chafing you." I remove them, then, grabbing a roll of duct tape off the bedside table, I loosely bind his ankles together. Throwing back the blankets, I stretch Rob out, slip in beside him, and cover us snugly.

"I should chain your neck to the headboard," I say. "But I won't, if you'll give me your word you won't try anything in the middle of the night."

"Try anything? The way you got me cuffed and taped?" Rob snorts. "Uh, I give you my word."

"Okay," I say. "But I should gag you just in case." I undo the bandana around his neck, tie a knot in the middle of it, and nudge the knot against his lips.

"Huh uh!" Rob shakes his head. "Not yet. Please? Later, okay? I'm not really sleepy. Could we just talk?"

"Talk? Sure." I tuck the gag beneath my pillow. We lie on our backs, a foot apart. Silence, except for the clicking of sleet.

"Icing up outside," I say.

"Yeah?" he says. "Yeah, I can hear it."

The silence extends. Rob rolls over, his back to me.

"So talk," I say. "Why do you want to talk? You're not going to talk me into letting you go."

"It's not that. I don't know. Because..." Voice trembling, he pauses, clears his throat, and continues in a firmer timbre. "I guess because I'm afraid I'll never get out of here alive, and, and talk helps distract me from that, and I guess I want to hear a human voice, I want someone to know me and hear me before... The silence and the cold in that room you've kept me in, it's like...a preview of my grave."

"Poor kid." I start to reach for him, then think better of it. "I'm sorry we had to do this. It was...unavoidable. Once the ransom comes..."

"That doesn't make any sense. My father doesn't have any money, and, as much as he and I fight"—Rob shakes his head and gives a low laugh—"I kind of wonder if he'd be willing to pay anything to get me back.

"I can tell you're sorry," he continues, "at the same time that you obviously enjoy having me here. You're my captor, but you seem to care about me, even though you could cut my throat at any time. Kinda crazy, isn't it?"

"I do care about you, and right now I really want to hold you," I admit, staring at the ceiling. "I don't know why I'm being so chivalrous. I don't know why I don't shove you onto your belly and take you good and hard right now."

"It's that kindness again. Second nature to you, even when you have so much power over me. Funny. Really funny."

"What's funny?" I snarl. "Are you mocking me? That's a damn-fool thing to do, considering the circumstances."

"Oh, no! No! That's not what I meant, dude! Oh, no!" Rob rolls over to face me. "I'm really thankful for your kindness. What's funny is...you've kidnapped me...and you've beat me...but, hell, as far as men go, you've been nicer to me than a lot of guys I've known. Certainly better than my father."

"Ah," I grunt, rage fading fast. "Your father?"

"I look up to him, don't get me wrong. I want to become a cop because he's a cop. And a damned good one. He's taught me to be strong. But he's like your buddy Jay. He's stern, he's mean. Bossy as fuck! Last man who took a belt to me—before you—was him. All through my childhood. For the smallest stupid infractions. He still makes fun of me because I read poetry. He thinks it's soft. Sissy stuff."

"Poetry? Really?"

"Now you're mocking me?" Rob chews his lip.

"No, I..." Reaching over, I grip his bruised shoulder.

He winces. "Ouch. Hurts!"

"Ah. Sorry. No, I meant, I read poetry to Jay all the time. I've actually gotten him to like it. Plath, Shakespeare, Whitman, Frost, Dickinson."

"Yeah, I like all those. And Kooser and Oliver and..."

He trails off. Firelight flickers over his blinded face. I touch his stubbly cheek. He starts. I touch his chest. He's shivering.

fog

"Are you warm enough?"

"N-no."

"You trembling because you're cold or because you're frightened?"

Rob clears his throat. "Both," he says huskily.

"Tonight, I'm just going to hold you. I promise. All right? Tomorrow might be another matter, but I know you're hurting from the beating right now, and from how Jay's used you. As much as I want you, I'm not a complete beast; I'm old enough to control myself if necessary. Tonight let's just cuddle, okay? It would make me very happy simply to hold you close till morning. That all right with you, Mr. Drake?"

"Yeah." Rob emits a long exhalation of breath. "O-okay."

"Come here, kid."

Rob scoots over. I wrap an arm around him and pull him closer still. He rests his head on my chest. I tuck the blankets more tightly about us. "How's that?"

"Good. You're really warm. And really hairy. Got some bear in your bloodlines?"

I guffaw. "Nothing like a big, bulky bear to keep a guy warm on a cold winter's night. Better than those skinny little girls you favor. Speaking of which, for a straight guy, you seem pretty easy with all this. My touch, I'm glad to say, doesn't seem to repulse you."

"Well, I guess it's the Scotch that helps me confess this, but..."

"But you've been with men before?

"Uhh. Umm. Sort of. Yeah. Experimented."

I chuckle. "Bi-curious, huh? Or bisexual?"

"I wouldn't say that."

"Whatever. I guess that helps explain why I don't have to pull Jay's knife to get you to sleep with me. What about Sarah? Does she know?"

"No, she doesn't. I like Sarah a lot, and who knows, maybe one day I'll get serious about her, but I've never been much on girls' company. Most of them are airheads. I kind of prefer to be around guys, you know?"

"Yes, I know," I say wryly. "Tell me about your experimentation then."

"Well, uhm. Okay. So, my first year in college, I had a really good buddy, Wes—he was older, mid-thirties, we used to play guitar together. He was tall, brawny, handsome, with long hair and a scruffy blond beard, sort of a power lifter gone to seed—and we drank a lot. A *lot*. An evening was a failure if we didn't get totally blasted. Wes, on a dare, he and I kissed one night at a bar. It sort of became a habit when we got shit-faced. Our friends thought it was funny. We fooled around some. Every now and then. But nobody knew that. We had girlfriends, of course—we both ran through lots of girls—but every now and then..."

"Fooled around? More than kissing?"

"Yeah. A few times...we got so drunk that... I don't remember all the details, but he blew me. A couple of times he played with my butt-hole and blew me. And a couple of times we passed out together, and in the mornings I jacked him off. And once...we, uh, sixty-nined."

"Really? It felt good?"

"From what I remember." Rob's voice is soft. "Felt real nice. Didn't taste bad either. He even swallowed, but I wasn't ready to do that."

"But your butt...? You all never...?"

"No. No." Rob's voice is deep and sad. "I lost my cherry my first night here." He clears his throat. "If it had to happen, I wish it'd been you, not Jay."

"Damn, boy," I whisper, stroking his hair. "Me too."

From a far distance, a train whistle sounds. Wind picks up, roaring in the chimney, making the house creak.

"Oh, God," Rob gasps. His shivering begins anew. "Sounds like death. Doesn't it sound like death to you?"

"It's just a train, kid. And the storm." I stroke his hair.

Rob snuggles closer; his cuffed hands brush my belly hair. "Please don't kill me. Please, Al?" His voice breaks. "Please? I haven't done anything to you. I'll do whatever you tell me to. Do whatever you want with me. I won't give you any fight. Just, when you're done with me, please let me go home."

I don't know how to reply. Instead of speaking, I hug him hard.

"Please?" He sniffles.

"I can't promise anything. Enough talk, kid. It's time for your gag," I say, mustering the old façade of sternness. I fetch the bandana from beneath the pillow. Gently, firmly, I push the knot into his mouth and tie the ends behind his head. He gives me no fight; instead, he starts to cry. I roll us onto our sides, wrap him in my arms, and rock him till he sobs himself to sleep.

chapter eighteen

I WAKE ONCE during the night, to Rob tugging on my hand. "Pith?" he mumbles. The wind's still howling outside. I help him hop on bound feet down the hall to the toilet. We relieve ourselves; I help him hop back. He curls inside my arms and falls asleep within a minute.

Dawn's dim light wakes me. We're lying on our backs, Rob's head on my shoulder. I pull back the covers and study my prisoner's young body: the defined muscles, the knife-scored skin, the bruise-blots, the long cock, half-hard with morning. This is, most likely, his prime. This is as close to perfection as he'll get. It's a zenith and a ripeness that mustn't be wasted. Especially if I can't convince Jay to release him unharmed.

No. No. I'll convince Jay. I kiss Rob's brow, then his gagged mouth, then his chin, then his mouth again, then the tape across his chest, then a pink nipple. I won't let Jay destroy this boy, despite all his reasons for revenge and malice. This son shouldn't have to suffer for his father's sins. Somewhere I need to muster the strength to resist Jay, to help us all move on. And where I'll find that strength, I think—if I find it anywhere—is in how Rob's bruised and helpless body makes me feel. I will not allow this boy's sublime flesh to end up rotting in a shallow grave in the spruce woods. I won't see such a youth ended in such a savage way.

My kisses are more determined now, ranging over Rob's face and torso. My cock's stiff and throbbing. Beneath my continuing attentions, Rob shifts and groans.

"Rob? You awake?"

He stretches and mumbles.

"I can't wait any longer. You understand?"

He lifts his head; his form goes taut. "Uh?"

"Let me know if I hurt you, if I do something you really don't like." I take his cuffed hands in mine. "I'm asking your permission. To make love to you."

He's silent for a moment, hesitating, no doubt weighing his options. Then, to my relief, he lies back and nods.

I'm trembling all over, with a desire I've held back for months on end. This must be something of what lightning feels, streaking toward the earth, or floodwater behind a crumbling dam. With a deep sigh, I lie on top of Rob, my cock rubbing his thigh, and I begin.

chapter nineteen

I LICK AND suck his nipples for a long time. An old line of poetry makes me smile in the midst of my delight: "An hundred years should go to praise / Thine eyes, and on thy forehead gaze; / Two hundred to adore each breast." Yes, yes, my coy captive. The small nubs are hard beneath my tongue, between my teeth, and Rob's moans appear to be proof of sheer pleasure. That, and the way he nods and arches his chest against my face, and the way, when I grip his cock, he thrusts into my fist. The rougher I work his nipples and pecs, the more aroused he appears to become.

I move lower, unwilling to wait any longer to taste his pretty cut prick. The ruddy cockhead's oozing copious precum; it trickles down the veiny shaft. He gasps as I lap the head, nibble the glans, and lick up the clear seeping. He whimpers as I start a fierce suction and tight-lipped bobbing. I suck him till he's close—twenty-two-year-olds don't take a lot of skill or a lot of time to get off—till he's bucking into my mouth and whining, his pubic hair matted with my drool.

"Not yet, kid," I say, pulling off. I give his spit-wet cock a sharp squeeze before cutting the tape binding his ankles. "Roll over."

"Uh? Uh?"

"No, I'm not going to fuck you. Roll over now. And spread your legs."

Rob does as he's ordered. My fingers range over his hard buttocks, over the swollen skin and black bruises my belt left.

"I'm sorry I had to hurt you," I say. My lips follow after my fingers, kissing each dark cloud that stains his white flesh. I take his ass-cheeks in my palms, massaging them softly, then even more softly I work a finger between them and brush the hair there.

Rob moans against the bed and shakes his head. "Plee, nah," he begs around the bandana's knot.

"Easy, easy," I say, finding the moist aperture and stroking it. "I know you're still hurting here. I know that Jay used your asshole to give you pain, but I want to use it to give you pleasure." I lift my finger to my mouth and wet it. I tickle the hole, tug at its thicket of hair, and rub it delicately. "Do you believe I can do that?"

"Uh huh," Rob mumbles.

"Does that feel good?" I push the very tip of my finger inside him.

Rob goes tense, then gradually relaxes. I move my finger around, in and out, around. I push in a fraction deeper.

"Does that hurt?"

"Nah."

"Can you take a little more?"

"Uh huh."

"Rob, boy, I've had a lot of practice making love to men. I really know how to make a guy's asshole feel great. Do you want me to make love to your butt? As long as I don't hurt you?"

"Plee. Yah. Pleeth." Gag or not, my captive manages to make his welcome clear.

I nudge his thighs wider, lie down on my belly between his legs, and spread his bruised cheeks. "I've been wanting to eat your butt since the first day I saw you," I growl. The crotch- and ass-scents are intense after Rob's near-week unwashed, but that's just fine with me. I tongue-bathe his crack from top to bottom, lapping up the sweat and the musk, before spreading his muscle-firm cheeks wider. Here's his hidden hole, his most vulnerable place, a pink clenching like a new bud, a wild rose. "Gather ye rosebuds while ye may," said the poet. Indeed. And as cruelly as Jay used this sweet little spot, some tenderer-than-usual attentions are called for. I circle the tiny aperture with my tongue, lick it up and down, then push the tip of my tongue into it as far as its shy tightness allows me.

Rob's whimpering into the sheets. His hole's slightly sugary, an earthy flavor like sorghum or dark bread. He bucks back against my mouth; I tug at his crack-hair with my teeth, nestle my face between his cheeks, and tongue-dig deeper.

"You like this?" I ask, ceasing my feast long enough to brush my beard across his buttocks.

"Yahhh." His nod's a shy enthusiasm.

"Want more?"

"Yaahhh." His rump bumps my face.

"Good boy," I chuckle. "Damn, you taste good." Spreading his puckered pink with my thumbs, I burrow even deeper.

He's ready for further explorations now, I think, after long minutes of my ardent rimming. Rolling Rob onto his back, I lift his furry legs onto my shoulders. To my triumphant delight, his cock is fully stiff. I grab lube, applying the gel to my forefinger and his hole. "Tell me if I hurt you," I order, before edging my fingertip in. When he doesn't protest, I push in a little farther, a little farther. I look up at him. His forehead's furrowed, his teeth sunk in the gag-knot.

"Good?"

"Yahh." He's trembling now, but around the cloth he gives me a feeble grin.

With that, I slide my forefinger up inside him as far as I can. He gasps; the knot of his hole clamps down on my digit. "Easy," I whisper. "I'm going to stop now and let you get used to me inside you. I won't continue until you tell me to."

We stay like that for a while, Rob's legs resting on my shoulders, my finger buried to the hilt inside his asshole. He trembles and pants; outside, the wind continues its wailing; beneath my breastbone, my heart's thumping with the mad excitement of a lover who's being given all he's ever ached for.

"Here," I say, nudging his erection into one cuffed hand. "Work yourself."

Rob obeys, stroking his shaft. He thrusts into his fist, huffing lightly around the bandana.

"Ready for more?"

"Yah."

Slipping my finger out, I add more lube. I stroke his wet entrance, then slide all the way in again. I start a slow rhythm to match his cock-jacking. He's shaking violently now. His legs slip off my shoulders and tauten around my waist, pulling me closer.

"Think you can take a second finger?"

Rob nods. I take my time. He winces, tenses, relaxes, sighs. Now my middle finger's joined my index finger up inside him, pumping gently. We rock together; his hole squeezes my fingers, loosens, squeezes, loosens, squeezes.

"You have a secret," I say. "Inside you."

"Um?" Rob cocks his head, clearly confused.

I pull out again, add yet more lube, enter him again with only my forefinger. This time I focus on the hard lump of his prostate. "Here," I say, rubbing it.

"UM!" Rob gasps and jerks. He shudders, locking his calves even more tightly around me. "UMM!" Above the strip of tape covering his eyes, his forehead knits up with shock.

"No one ever fooled with that before?" I laugh, fingering his tiny seat of ecstasy with a soft but steady prodding. "That's your prostate. Like that, huh?"

"Umm HUH!" Rob's head bobs; he jacks his dick even harder; he squirms against me.

"I told you I knew how to make love to a man's ass." I push my finger in a fraction farther, rub his prostate harder. His breath catches; he emits a little sob.

Long sweet minutes pass. I massage him inside till he's half-wild, moaning and writhing with obvious rapture, thighs straining, hand a blur around his long cock.

"Want to cum?" I say, lapping his cockhead. "I think you need to cum."

"Uhhm! UHHMM!" Rob nods, frantic, bouncing on the bed.

"You got it, bud." Pushing his hand aside, I swallow his cock. Rob shouts, his fingers pulling at my hair. I finger-fuck him hard now, I suck him hard, running my tongue up and down his shaft, giving his cockhead a few quick, shallow bobs, then deep-throating him till I can barely breathe.

It only takes half a minute of combined cock- and ass-work before my handsome prisoner's done. Roaring, he clutches the back of my head and spurts into my mouth, his butthole spasming around my finger. Three huge jets, thick and faintly sweet. I have to gulp fast to keep from spilling them. Can't remember when I took so much tasty cum.

I sit up and slowly slide my finger from Rob's asshole. He sprawls limply on his back, gasping around his gag. He grips his dick and squeezes. A last gob wells out. "Can't waste that," I say, licking it off. He jolts and giggles.

"Did you enjoy yourself?"

Rob manages a weak thumb's up before rolling onto his side.

"Want to sleep some more?"

"Uhhhhh huhhhhhh."

"Do you need to piss?"

"Nah."

I cover him with blankets, sit beside him, and caress his face. "It's barely daybreak. I'll get you up later. Maybe make us some buckwheat cakes and sausage."

Rob nods sleepily.

"Rob." I take a deep breath. "You know that sooner or later I'm going to fuck you. I'll be very easy, very gentle. I'll screw you real slow. I'll do my best to make you feel good, to make you feel as good as I did just now. I'll do my best not to hurt you like Jay did. But I want to... I've got to be inside you. I need to...take you like that. To possess you that way. Whether you want me to or not. You understand?"

Rob lifts his head from the pillow. "Uh," he grunts. He lies back, inhales, and nods.

"You won't fight me?"

He grits the knot between his teeth, then his mouth falls slack. "Nah."

"And you believe me when I say I won't hurt you?"

"Yeh."

Bending, I kiss him. I tongue his lips, the sodden cloth gagging him, his stubbly chin. Then I rise, tucking him in more tightly. Against the window, upon the tin roof, the ice storm Jay had warned me about has begun in earnest, hard ticking of crystals like an impatient clock, like a predator's claws.

At the door I look back. Rob's curled up like a child again, dead to the world.

chapter twenty

"WHY DID JAY cry the other night?" Rob mumbles in between sorghum-topped bites of buckwheat cakes. "When he was fucking me and cutting me? I could feel droplets of hot water falling on me. Those were his tears, right?"

We're on the couch again, before another wood fire. Outside, the ice storm is covering everything—porch steps, hood of my truck, boughs of spruce, gravel drive—with a slick sheet of crystal. We won't be going anywhere for a while. Glad I stocked up on food yesterday.

"I don't really know. Why did you cry?" I counter. "I know his cock is really big, really thick. It hurt you bad, I guess."

"No. Well, at first. When he first pushed it up in me, it hurt like hell despite the drugged haze I was in. But for some reason or another, he went very, very slow. It's as if that first night, he really wanted to hurt me, but that second night, he was doing his best *not* to hurt me, to let my ass get used to it. The lube made a huge difference. And after a while I did sort of get used to it. It was uncomfortable, but it wasn't agony.

He kept whispering, 'I know how you feel, boy. I know how you feel.'"

Rob licks sorghum off his lips and shakes his head. "I was crying, well, because, even as drugged up as I was, I was scared—to be so helpless, to be totally at a hostile stranger's mercy. I'm scared still, as nice as you're being to me. Wouldn't you be scared? Every now and then, he'd stroke me with that knife, I could feel how sharp it was, and I was afraid he was going to stab me, and I didn't want to die. I *don't* want to die. Mainly I was crying because, I don't know, I guess I just felt sad. Really sad. Sad for me, sad for you, even sad for him. Fuck, we're *all* so screwed-up."

I laugh low, patting his shoulder. "Truer words were never spoken, son. Makes sense. You're damned observant for your age. Keep talking and you'll have *me* crying. Open up, here's more pancake."

Rob takes another bite; I do the same. "I don't know exactly. Why Jay was crying. Here," I say, nudging a piece of sausage patty between his lips. "I have my suspicions, but that's not information you need to know."

Rob chews and swallows. "He was pretty drunk, I think."

"Jay drinks every evening. But then so do I. He's been through a lot, but, again, there are things you shouldn't know. Or see." I tap his blindfold. "For your own good."

"Yeah. Okay. But...is he on drugs? The guy seems kind of erratic. He was so brutal that first night—fuck, dude, he raped me with a bottle!—but then that next night he was kissing me and touching me like...a lover. A tender lover. Like I said, even when he, uh, entered me, he was gentle, like he was trying to make me enjoy it. The contrast was crazy. God, dude, please don't tell me I'm at the mercy of a drug addict."

"No. He knows I wouldn't tolerate it, though I think some of the guys he works with indulge in that fucking crystal meth. The little town we're near is full of dirt-poor people, and poverty breeds those kinds of habits. 'Drugs or Jesus,' that's a Tim McGraw song. When your life isn't for shit, you either get high or get religious."

I feed Rob another bite of pancake. "Mmm," he says, licking his lips.

"Good?"

"Yeah. For redneck food." Rob smiles thinly. "I'm *joking*. Yeah, it is. It's really good. Thank you. Other than the tape and rope and cuffs, you've been a splendid host. No wonder it's called Southern hospitality." One eyebrow arches over the duct tape, brown bird rising above layered fog. "I'm being only half-ironic, by the way. I'm damned tired of being bound up and having that fucking ball stuffed in my mouth again and again, and, yes, my butt hole is still a little sore, but the food's twice as good as what I'm used to. Sarah and I tend toward McDonalds and Burger King, which is nothing to write home about."

"Jay and I are more Sonic and Taco Bell guys, but I try to cook whenever time allows, or when we have guests. With all this ice coming down, we won't be indulging in fast food for a while. Even my 4x4 is no good on ice."

I take a bite of buckwheat cake and chew appreciatively. "This *is* pretty good. You're lucky to have a country cook for a captor." I pat Rob's flat belly and tug at the brown hairs below his navel. "You could afford to gain a few pounds."

Rob gives a blind grin. "Yeah. If I had to be taken, you'd be the kind of kidnapper I'd choose. What's that sweet stuff on the pancakes? It doesn't taste like syrup."

"Sorghum. Sort of like molasses. We used to make it from sugar cane when I was a kid in...well, the holler I grew up in."

"Sorghum? And you used to make it? God, you *are* country. Well, it's good."

Rob coughs. A nervous sound. Preparatory. Tentative. "Hey, Al?"

Beseeching. Pleading. The tone of his voice makes me feel like a benevolent king giving a long-awaited audience to supplicants. "Yes, Rob?"

"Is there any way you could take this tape off my eyes for a while? Give me a little break? Maybe while you wear your mask? Please? I've been blindfolded for days."

"Maybe. We'll see."

"And Al? I smell and I'm tired of smelling. Could I take a shower? Or a bath? Or, at the very least, could you clean me up some? Please?"

"I like the way you say 'Please.' Keep it up. And I love the way you smell. Your 'stink's' like an aphrodisiac to me. But, yeah, after so many days unbathed, I must admit you're getting a little rank, even for me. I'll wash you up later, I promise."

"Thank you. Thank you."

Rob falls silent. I add another dribble of sorghum to the cakes, give him another forkful, and take a bite myself. We chew side by side. The fire crackles and the ice clicks outside.

"Al?" Rob's voice is soft, sheepish. "If I said something, would you try not to assume that I'm lying or trying to manipulate you? To, uh, ingratiate myself?"

"*This* should be good. I'll try." I rise, emptied plates in hand.

"You did make me feel good. Last night. This morning? Hell, I'm blind. I have no idea what time of day it is. Anyway, you said you knew how to make a man feel...pleasure that way. I was sore there, and I didn't really think that you'd be able to...but you were right."

Rob's cheeks redden. He purses his lips and hangs his head. "I'd never been touched inside, there, and I've never had a blow job like that. I know it's as much about your pleasure as mine... I can tell by the way you touch me and kiss me how much you want me, how much you want to keep me...and you know I don't want to be here, and I'm still praying that you two have some mercy on me and let me loose in one piece... but, well, shit, I'm rambling."

He lifts his head in my direction. "What I mean to say is, I'm terrified—can you blame me?—but it helps, your touch helps me feel less afraid. At the same time that you've made me more helpless than I've ever been—I feel like a fucking child, all these years working out, preacher curls, bench presses, building muscle, trying to be brave, trying to be strong—and all it takes is a drug-soaked cloth over my face in the middle of a good long jog, some tape, and I'm vulnerable as a brat in a diaper..."

"You're still rambling," I say, placing the dishes on the coffee table and sitting beside him. I wrap an arm around him; instead of jolting or tensing, he leans into me.

"I'm trying to say that you've made me frightened and helpless, yeah, but you've also made me feel cared for, even cherished in some weird way. You've been better to me than my father. Or, hell, even Sarah. She's way too into the way she looks to touch me the way you do."

I give my boy a broad grin. I must look like a proud, happy fool. Glad he can't see me.

"Well, I've had a lot more practice making love to men than the little tartlets you normally sleep with. However, flattery will not get you free." I hug him hard and then rise. "But we'll see about that bath. You want to watch ESPN later? Oh, wait, guess you can't watch anything, huh? Let me think about the blindfold. You do like sports, right?"

"Yeah. Especially football and hockey."

"How about action movies?"

"Oh, yeah. *Dude* movies. The more violence the better."

"Sword-swinging? We got a bunch of those on DVD. *300. Gladiator. Braveheart. Alexander.*"

"What is this? The Bondage Bed and Breakfast?" Another thin smile. "Good meals, now movies? Later a bath? Sure, I love all those flicks."

"We have a little TV in the bedroom. Let me get some work done now. Later today, how about I bathe you? And after dinner, we can watch a movie."

Rob bows his head. "Your call, man. Whatever you say."

chapter twenty-one

ROB SPENDS THE day bound on the couch, snuggled peacefully beneath the afghan, the bandana knotted between his teeth. No pressing need to keep the boy forcibly silent—very little likelihood that anyone would show up, especially considering the dangerous weather, to overhear any noise he might make—so the gag's unnecessary, but I savor the feeling of power it gives me to control his speech.

Just across the room, I sit at my little desk, catching up on work online; got to keep the paychecks coming, as spotty as Jay's work schedule can be. Every now and then I add a log to the fire. Every now and then I look up from the screen to admire my hostage—the blinded, silenced face; the motionless form, athletic-looking even beneath the blanket. On the stove, I have yellow-eye beans soaking for dinner. Outside, ice continues to fall; branches dip lower and lower with the frozen weight. I take a brief break to feed us lunch—leftover chili and a quick pone of cornbread with apple butter—then reposition him on the couch. Now, as the gray day grows grayer with dusk, it's time for Rob's bath.

Up the stairs we shuffle. Side by side we stand in the bathroom's bright light. I remove his bandana gag and pull out scissors.

"I'm going to cut your tape bonds off. I guess I don't need to say—"

"No, dude, you don't need to say it. I swear I won't try to get away. And I won't touch my blindfold. You're bigger than me, I'll still be cuffed, you might have a knife or gun nearby. I'm no idiot. I remember that beating. I'll do whatever you say."

"Hold real still." I snip the tape and slowly peel off the strips circling his chest, arms, and back.

"Ouch!" he complains, flinching.

"Be thankful you don't have much in the way of chest hair, kid," I say. "Jay's taped me up a few times before he fucked me—we enjoy kink every now and then—and having the tape pulled off my chest and wrists hurt way worse than the ass-fucking."

"Yeah, I understand. It does hurt coming off my wrist- and ankle-hair." Unbound now, save for the handcuffs, Rob stretches. "Thanks, man. Nice change of pace. I haven't felt this free since you took me."

Shyly his hand gropes the air, settling on my forearm. "You're hairy as a bear," Rob says hoarsely. "I can't see you, of course, but I can feel it, all over your chest and belly. It's manly. When you hold me, it feels like I'm nestling in a fuzzy velour blanket. I like Sarah's softness, especially her breasts... but I like your hardness too. Hard muscles; thick, soft hair."

"Really? You like that?" I say, disbelieving.

"Yeah. Not what I'm used to, but, like I said earlier...a comfort. Being wrapped up in your arms is a helluva lot better than shivering in that back room or in the basement, that's for damn sure."

I want to say that he's sounding very much like a bisexual, which would make the whole situation easier on everybody, but I resist the urge. Instead I cup his right pec. "Like you, Rob. Hard muscles, soft skin."

"I always wanted to be hairy," he says, smiling, plucking at the sparse brown strands rimming his nipples, "but this is all I got. You, you're hairy and you're strong. I've tried all my life to be stronger. To be tougher. I admire strength. You and I, we could have been buddies if we'd met in some other way."

I stroke those fine tendrils around his nipples. "Did you just give me a compliment? You're all flattery today."

Another shrug, which in any other circumstance might be called insouciant. "How about that bath?"

"Shower, actually. I'm going to join you."

Yet another shrug. "You're in charge. If it weren't for the fact that I'm afraid your friend will pop some pills, fuck me till I'm bloody, shoot me through the head, and dump my body in a landfill..." He shudders. "If it weren't for all that, I'd be enjoying the good food and warm bed and, and blow-jobs and all that other...and giving up control for a while. Fuck..." Rob gives his head a slow shake. "Don't you get tired of being a man all the time? Tough all the time? Always got to take charge. Fighting, fighting..."

"Shhh." I turn the water on, adjust the temperature, then loop a short length of rope around Rob's cuffed wrists. "Yeah, I know what you mean. So you know I'm going to take care of you, right? You trust me to be good to you as long as you behave, right?"

"Yes," Rob whispers. "I do. I...do. Don't know how it's happened"—he shakes his head with apparent surprise—"but I do."

"So you're tired of fighting? Don't fight this. Watch your step," I say, leading him into the shower stall by the tether. He gasps as the warm water hits him in the chest and sluices over his loins. "Arms up," I say, tugging. When he obeys, I tie his hands above his head, anchoring the rope to a pipe.

"All right? Comfortable?"

Rob nods. "Yeah. The water feels wonderful."

Fetching washcloth and soap, I begin. I scrub the remaining tape-adhesive from his face. I scrub the smelly brown moss of his armpits. I scrub tape-adhesive off his knife-marked chest. I take his flaccid cock and balls in my hands, very gently soaping them up. I turn him. He groans—a sound, for once, of contentment, not discomfort—head sagging beneath the spray. I scrub more adhesive off his broad, tattooed back and the cross that Jay knife-cut there. I spread his belt-bruised buttocks, cleaning the crack, its dense fuzz. I soap up his long, hairy legs. Falling to my knees, I wash his white feet.

"Done," I say, giving his cock a quick kiss as I rise. I move him in a slow circle beneath the water till he's well rinsed.

"Oh, thanks. Oh, thanks! God," Rob mutters, flashing a drowsy smile. His pale skin is flushed a faint pink.

"My turn." I soap and scrub myself. "Hell, I'm almost as aromatic as you were. Jay's always loved my musk. He's always said a strong scent is proof of a man's high testosterone level."

"Then that makes us both studs." Rob leans against the shower stall, chin on his chest, sinewy arms flexing above his head.

I rinse, then stand before him in the shower spray, water streaming down my belly. I study him, my cock rising fast. "You're getting quite the whiskers, kid." I touch his roughening cheek. "We've only had you a few days, and already you've got a nice start on a beard."

"Testosterone." Rob grins sadly. "Go ahead."

"What?"

"I can tell by the tone of your voice. You want to touch me again. Go ahead. Just if...if you fuck me, please, man, go easy. My hole still aches some."

"I'm not going to fuck you now." I swallow hard. "But I am before Jay gets home. Tonight or tomorrow."

Rob nods. "Yes. Okay. I guess I kind of knew that already."

I wrap my arms around him, pulling him back into the cascade of water. He lifts his head. I stroke his wet hair, and then I kiss him. To my delight, he kisses me back.

We stand there for a long time beneath the spray, kissing gently, our tongues sliding over one another. I jack him till he's hard, till he's tugging on the rope above his head and panting against my mouth; I drop to my knees and I suck his cock; I turn him, spread his ass-cheeks, lap his hole till the pipe he's bound to rattles with his happy rocking; I turn him, suck his prick again, edge him with my mouth and tongue till he's so close to climax he's whining.

"Oh. Oh! Al, oh! Finish me, dude? Please, dude! Please?"

"Sorry, kid. Not yet." I rise and we kiss some more, tenderly, little laps and nibbles, his tongue running over my chin, my teeth tugging his lower lip.

"Wow. It's as sweet as kissing Wes," Rob murmurs.

"It's about cocktail time," I say. I squeeze his cock and jack it again; he shudders and bucks and nods.

"Damn, dude. You're a real tease," he whines as I drop his dick, leaving it to bob in the steam, just short of shooting. Unknotting his hands from the pipe, I lead my blind slave from the shower, dry him off, dress myself in a fresh pair of boxer briefs, sweatpants, moccasins, and hoodie, and lead his naked and sightless stagger downstairs. Faulkner's whiskey sours await.

chapter twenty-two

"WHAT THE FUCK?" Rob sighs. "This is crazy." Leaning against me, he slurps the drink I lift to his mouth.

Rob's secured again. His hands are cuffed in his lap. Rope crisscrosses his chest, securing his big arms to his sides, and binds his ankles together. I've got the fire heaped with wood, cabbage frying in bacon grease, and yellow-eye beans simmering on the stove. New Age music—the kind I play when I'm stressed or when I want to feel cozy, safe, and remote from the world and its consequences—pours softly from the iPod dock. The ice continues to fall; the TV warns of local power outages.

"Crazy? What's crazy?" I gulp the last of the whiskey sour and clink the ice against the glass. "You want another?"

"Yes. Please." Rob's head falls back against the couch. "What's crazy is that you've taken me by force and you're holding me here against my will, but we just necked in the shower like fucking newlyweds. You're probably the best, the most passionate kisser I've ever encountered, and you certainly give the best blow job I've ever enjoyed. I must be losing my mind. Maybe I *am* bisexual. Shit. What are you putting in these goddamn drinks? Are you drugging me again?"

I pat Rob's head. "Keep talking. Like I said, flattery won't free you, but, well, keep talking. You can't see me, but I'm beaming."

Right now I'm entirely happy. I'm so happy that I wish the ice outside would never stop and that Rob and I could stay here forever. Jay, my sweet, vicious, controlling, vengeful, hairy, maimed, thick-dicked, brutal Top-Man Jay, seems so far away it's as if he were only some vague character from a novel I read in my adolescence. With Jay, I'm always obeying him, always worried about his unpredictable behavior and his occasionally unreasonable reactions to the smallest things, always excusing his bossy, selfish demeanor by remembering what he'd suffered in prison. With Rob, well, it's damned fine to be the Top, the Daddy, the one calling the shots.

"It's just insane," Rob says. "That's all I'm saying. It's got to be some version of Stockholm Syndrome. You know, where the captive gets weirdly attached to his captor?"

"Whatever it is, it makes your time here less horrible, right?"

"Yeah. Right. Less horrible. At least till your buddy gets back. Hell, with him and his meanness gone, it's like a sex and food vacation. To be honest, uh, Sarah doesn't put out as often as I'd like."

"Does she suck your dick?"

"Once in a rare while."

"Not as well as I do?"

"God, no. She doesn't really like to do it."

"She doesn't like to suck your dick? She's crazy. Does she eat your ass? Or work that sweet spot up inside you, your prostate?"

"*God*, no."

"And you've enjoyed all that with me?" I pull his head against mine.

"Dude," Rob says. "Yes. V-very much. Despite the, uh, unfortunate circumstances. You make me—make my body—feel even better than Wes did."

"Good. Stay here and keep cozy. I'll make another drink."

We're warm on whiskey and more Shiraz by the time dinner's ready. I feed Rob spoonfuls of beans with chowchow, forkfuls of cabbage, hunks of leftover pone smeared with butter and honey. He grunts with appreciation, then timidly asks for a second helping: "Please, sir...may I have some... more?"

"Ha! Dickens." I slap his shoulder and oblige. We're both full and drunk by the time I rinse off the dirty dishes. For another hour we sit quietly by the fire, Rob's head in my lap, listening to the music. We split a piece of cake and ice cream. He talks about his childhood, his college classes, his gymnastic awards, how much he misses his late mother. "How about a movie in bed?" I ask. It's just then that there's a crash outside in the forest surrounding the house. The music stops; the few dim lights I've left burning snick off.

chapter twenty-three

"POWER'S OUT THROUGHOUT the house," I growl, returning from my reconnoitering. Freeing Rob's feet, I lead him up the staircase by candlelight. "Thank God we have a gas fireplace, a gas stovetop, a wood fireplace, a full woodshed, and a recently stocked pantry. We can store food out on the porch, if need be. Don't worry, kid, I'll keep you warm and fed."

"Somehow I don't doubt that. Ow! Shit! My toe!"

"Oh, damn. Sorry. Easy now. I got you. Careful." I maneuver my blindfolded boy up the last steps, into the bathroom for a pre-sleep piss, and then into my bed, where I rope his ankles together before tucking him in. I start the gas fire, light candles, and join him beneath the blankets.

"Al. Would you... I don't mean to be pushy, but, my blindfold? Please, would you give me a little break? The tape's wet from the shower, it's itching, it smells... Please?"

"All right. Let me put on my mask. Wait here."

"Okay, I guess I'll wait here," Rob says, flashing me a crooked smile. He wiggles his cuffed hands beneath the blanket, then his bound feet. "Guess I won't take a walk around the property. Or lift weights. Or jog down the icy hill shouting for help."

"Smartass brat. Watch yourself. I enjoyed belting your splendid butt before, and I'd be more than glad to belt it again." I give the side of his head a carefully measured slap. "Pretty as it is, in my opinion your ass looks even better bruised up." Retrieving the leather half-hood from a drawer beside the bed, I wiggle it over my head till the eye-holes are aligned right. Quick scan of the room. Too dark to see much. All the distinctive pictures—not many, since neither Jay nor I give a flying rat's ass about decorating—I take down or turn over. Now it's just a room with a couple of windows, a fireplace, a closet, a bed, and a dresser. No identifying details for Rob to make note of.

From the dresser I lift Jay's black knife. "Okay, pretty boy," I say, kissing his unshaven cheek. Using pillows, I prop him up against the headboard; the blanket falls to his waist, exposing his rope-wrapped chest. "Here we go. Keep still."

I apply the knife just behind his left ear, slicing the tape with great caution from top to bottom. Then I peel it off, first from the back of his buzz-cut, then around his face, uncovering the right eye, then the left.

Done. The tape hangs from my hand. Rob looks up at me, blinking. In the restless candlelight, his eyes are wide and blue, his lashes long and brown. He doesn't look around the room, trying to gauge his surroundings. He looks directly at me. His lips quiver; his eyes grow wet; he smiles.

"Hey," he says, wonder in his voice. "Wow," he says. "Thank you so much." He squints, clenches his eyes shut, then opens them again. "I feel a little like Lazarus."

"What do you see?" I sheathe the black blade and put it in the bedside table; don't want to scare him more than necessary. "Might as well take notes for future reference. If you ever get to a police station."

Rob looks at the room now, turning his head this way and that. His eyes return to me. "Nothing of use. Could be any room in any old house out in the country. All I see is you."

I stand beside him, dropping a hand on his naked shoulder. "I know. Mask or not, I'm taking a risk here. What do you see, seeing me?"

"You're bigger than I imagined. Bigger chest. Great beard. Wish I could grow a beard like that. You look like a Civil War re-enactor."

I chuckle. "Well, I did have a few ferocious Rebel forebears. What else?"

"Promise you won't get angry?"

"Oh, hell, I don't like the sound of that. You're always asking me that. Okay, I promise."

"A redneck, yeah. But one with—come closer."

I take a step nearer and bend down to him, till our faces are mere inches apart. His breath's tinged with whiskey.

"If I'd seen you when you took me, I would have shit myself. You look mean. Really good-looking, from what I can tell, but mean. The shoulders, the chest, the gut, the bushy beard...you look like a wrestler. Like a guy no one would have the balls to cross. But now..."

Rob stares at me steadily. His lashes are long and wet, glistening. "You have kind eyes. No surprise there, considering the way you hold me. You look like a big fucking take-no-shit biker-dude, until I get closer and see that softness inside your eyes."

"Softness?" I growl.

"Yeah," Rob nods. "No way around it. Nothing unmanly, dude. You're all man, no doubt. I mean kindness. Conflicted, sure. But it's loving, it's kindness. If...if I get out of here alive, it'll be due to that." He looks away, chews his lower lip, then returns his gaze to my masked face. "If I don't, it'll...be because that kindness failed."

"Oh, fuck. Oh, great. Thanks a lot. I'm gonna get some Scotch," I rasp. "You'll keep nice and quiet, right? No need to gag you just yet?"

"Naw." Rob smiles up at me. He blinks; a tear rolls down his cheek, then another. "Shit. Oh, God, I'm sorry. I try to be brave, but I'm so afraid." Turning his head, he wipes his face against a pillow. "I'll be quiet."

I sit in the cold kitchen for a long time, sipping Famous Grouse in the dark, listening to ice click and crack. After a while, I unlock the door and step out onto the porch. I break off an icicle from the eaves and lick its sharp clarity. The cove's white, every surface encapsulated in freeze. I break the icicle in half, toss it into the yard, step back inside, lock the door, and trudge back upstairs.

Rob's lying on his side in the flicker of gas-fire and candle-flame. His eyes are still wet, but drowsy too. His chest is still uncovered, the blankets tangled about his waist. "Where have you been?" he whispers, sitting up.

"Drinking. Went outside to see how bad the ice is."

"Did I hurt you?"

"Hurt me? No. Hell, no. You're helpless. You can't hurt me. Here." I lift Rob's head with one hand, giving him a sip of Scotch with the other.

Now I stand before the fire. Sound of the far train again. No wind tonight. Just the snap and tick of falling ice and, behind and beneath that, stillness, a wintry paralysis.

"Are you sleepy?" Rob says behind me.

"No."

"I'm cold, Al. Come on in."

I turn. I sit on the bed beside him. I take a cuffed hand in mine. I stare at the fire, and then I stare at the blankets covering his lower body, and then I bring myself to gaze at him. "It's good to see your eyes again," I say. "I used to watch you at that Mexican restaurant by the river. I was there the day you jumped in to save that drowning pigeon; I saw the way your wet tank top clung to your nipples. You used to get so drunk on margaritas, cutting up like a little boy with your friends. I used to watch the way your tight t-shirts showed off the curves of your chest, the way your biceps bulged when you stretched, the hair on your forearms...brown in the shade but golden in the sunlight. And those gym shorts you wore sometimes, without underwear...the bulge there, the swing of your dick, the plump curve of your ass...all that rich, fucking lovely fur on your calves. And those little goatees you kept growing and shaving off. And these blue eyes." I cup his face in my hands.

"You fell in love with me."

"Yes." My turn to hang my head helplessly.

"Take off your clothes, Al, big mean redneck captor. Get in here and hold me."

I lift my head and stare at him.

"Yeah. You heard right." Tipping toward me, he wiggles his arms beneath the rope till he can touch my side with a finger.

"Why are you doing this, Rob?" I pull his face closer to mine. "Asking me to hold you and to bed you? What about Sarah? What about your supposed heterosexuality?"

"I don't know why. Yeah, I do. I think I'm going to die soon, and I want to feel as much, I want to touch and be touched as much as I can before then. Sarah isn't here, and neither is your guy Jay. Just you and me and the fire inside and the ice outside. Does that make sense?"

"Yes."

"I know you can't promise me anything; you can't promise to release me unharmed." Rob's eyes once again are welling with tears, and once again his voice is shaking. "I'd ask you to let me go before Jay gets back, but I know you won't. You can't. In fact, you don't want to. You want to keep me here. You like me naked, bound, and at your mercy. And if you gave me my life back, you might lose yours. I understand that. So, since I probably won't get out of here alive, I want to make love in as many ways as we can before I rot in whatever hole I end up dumped in."

I nod, rising, fighting back my own tears. Rob leans back into the pillows and watches as I strip in the firelight. Naked, penis half-erect, I sit on the bed's edge again and give him a sip of Scotch before taking one myself. "Damn," he says, wide eyes ranging over my torso, then down to my cock. He wipes his face against the pillow again and shakes his head.

"Son, if you like this," I chuckle, "you gotta be bi, 'cause there ain't nothing womanly about me...except my heart, I guess." I give my fur-matted chest a rub, then my matted beer-belly, then my swaying prick.

"You're hung, dude. And so hairy I can hardly see your skin," Rob says, grinning. "And, well, you've got the kind of muscles I've always wanted. I told you I admire strength! No wonder you wrestled me down so easily when Jay's buddies came by."

"I'm as much fat as I am muscle. So is Jay. Fast food and beer... You, on the other hand, not a shred of fat on you." I run a finger along Rob's ridged stomach. "I drink too many six-packs to have a six-pack."

"Hell, I'd give a lot for your bulk and maturity."

"And I'd give a lot for your lean, fit youth. Hell, look here." I tug regretfully at the gray hairs between my pecs, then at the gray on my chin.

"You're prime, I'd say. Ripe."

I take the last sip of Scotch. "*You're* prime, I'd say. I'm just an ole bear heading over the hill. Roll over." When Rob does, I cover us and spoon him from behind.

"I can feel your hard-on against my butt," Rob says. "Is tonight the night? Christ, dude, go slow! It's hard to imagine something so big going up my—"

In answer, I clap my left hand firmly over his mouth and with the other I position my cockhead against his butt-crack. Rob lies there, uncomplaining, as I thrust against him.

"I want inside you so bad," I whisper. Rob nods and grunts.

"I'll be real careful, real slow," I say. Reaching around him, I clasp his cock. It's half-hard. A few short strokes, and it's erect, pulsing in my palm.

"I'm going to take you now, kid. All right? I'm going to eat your ass again, open you up slow with my tongue, and then I'm going to fuck you. I'll use lots of lube. I'm going to cum up your ass and jack you off. It's time, isn't it? It's time."

Rob nods. To my delight, he cocks his butt and nudges it back against my groin, then thrusts his hard-on into my hand.

I sigh, pilgrim topping the hill, looking down the long slope into the Promised Land. And that's when, in the pile of clothes I shucked onto the floor, my goddamn cell phone chirps.

chapter twenty-four

Jay's manic, more so than I've ever heard him. He chatters on and on about the hot nightlife in Richmond. Apparently he's witnessing it first-hand—the sounds behind him are distinctly that of a crowded bar, with loud music, shouted conversations, and the clinking of glasses. "Good business connections," he yells, "lots of deals made." The phrase he keeps repeating is "bad ice storm." I can barely make out what he says. When I hang up, I know one thing—he won't be home any time soon, due to the weather, the state of emergency, and closed interstates—and I suspect another thing—his brain's soaking in more than just booze tonight. Those trashy motherfuckers he works with have given him some of their fucking drugs.

Rob's already frightened enough of Jay, so I don't mention the latter suspicion. The former fact, Jay's extended absence, inspires in Rob, as I would have predicted, visible relief. "That's good news," he says frankly. "Did he say anything about the ransom? Has my father gotten the money yet?"

"No, no word about that. Just that the roads are too bad to travel. He'll be in Richmond for several more days, unless we get a major thaw."

I pat Rob's bare flank. "Your asshole just got a reprieve. Unbelievably, as hot as you are and as much as I want up your butt, as long as I've waited...suddenly I'm not in the mood. I have some things to think about. But you..."

I turn off the gas fireplace. From the roll of duct tape on the dresser, I pull off a strip, press it over Rob's mouth, and smooth it over his lips. "You can take this for a while? You can breathe all right?"

Rob nods. "Um hm."

"You get some sleep, okay?" I say, tucking him in and pulling on my clothes. "I'm going downstairs to read. I'll be up later. If you need me, shout as best you can. I'll hear you."

Rob blinks up at me, blue eyes soft, a glance that, in some other context, could almost be described as doting. He nods, closing his eyes.

Downstairs, I lie on the couch, reading Faulkner till my eyes are tired. After a few chapters, I turn off the lamp and try to sleep. Instead, my anxiety starts counting the number of chemicals I've heard are rampant in town, drugs Jay might be indulging in. Crystal meth, oxycontin, heroin. Maybe cocaine, maybe speed. Shit, fuck, shit.

I drowse off, then wake with a jolt to the distant snapping and crashing of woodland branches, brought down by the weight of ice. Stiffly, I shuffle up to the toilet, then into the bedroom, where I strip. Rob's snoring, back to me. He wakes as I climb in beside him. He rolls over. I kiss his taped mouth. He rests his head on my shoulder, snuggling against me like a child, and starts snoring again. I lie there, an arm around him, staring at the ceiling for a long time before falling asleep.

chapter twenty-five

ROB'S WRAPPED TIGHTLY in my arms when I wake. I pull back the blankets to marvel at his nakedness, but last night's worries are as sharp and salient as my desire for my sleeping hostage.

"Mm?" Rob grunts against the tape as I slip out of bed. He rolls onto his back, cocking a quizzical eyebrow.

"Stay there," I say gruffly. "I have lots of work to do; I've got a lot on my mind."

He nods, gazing sleepily up at me. I pull on my lounge clothes. "I didn't mean to be brusque," I say at the door. "I'm just worried about Jay getting home on bad roads. I'll make us breakfast in a little bit."

I'm at my computer before I realize I can't do any work; there's no damned electricity. Cursing, I pull on boots and fetch a few armloads of wood from the shed. The ground's treacherous with ice; three times I almost slip and fall. At least it's warming up; the icefall has turned to steady rain.

Coffee next. Got to use the old stovetop pot. While it brews, I fry and flip scrapple, trying to remember the signs of drug use. No luck. I don't know jack shit about drug culture, other than the marijuana that Jay brings home occasionally. Sharing a bong with him has been just about the entirety of my drug experiences.

Other than caffeine, of course. I pour a cup before slipping the crisp slices of scrapple onto a plate. Time to check on my handsome prisoner, my hill-country version of Sleeping Beauty. "Boy, want some breakfast?" I shout up the stairs.

No answer.

"Rob? Are you all right?"

Worried, I climb the steps, lope down the hall, splashing coffee in my wake, and throw open the bedroom door. To my surprise, I find Rob lying on his back, covers down to his thighs, cuffed hands fondling his full erection. His eyebrows arch; beneath the tape, the line of his lips curves into a smile.

"Uh," I say. I place the coffee cup on the dresser. I watch him tug on his shaft, squeeze his balls, finger the head. My cock tents my sweatpants in response.

"You little bastard. Goddamn you. You're so fucking beautiful. You know the power your body has over me, don't you?"

Rob nods; lazily he works himself.

"So you've somehow gone from a weeping, terrified kidnap victim to a cock-tease within a week?"

Rob nods.

"Because you think you can convince me to free you?"

"Huh uh," Rob grunts, shaking his head. There's hopelessness in that small sound, that mundane movement.

"*Carpe diem*? Because you're afraid to die?"

Rob pauses only for a moment before continuing his deliberate strokes and giving me another nod. His blue eyes are wide, desperate.

I jerk off my clothes, climb onto the bed, and lie on top of him. When I peel the tape off his mouth, he winces, giving a little squeal of discomfort.

"That's what you get for growing such a fine beard so damned fast," I say before pushing my mouth against his. Our kisses are harder this time. He squirms beneath me, biting my lower lip till it hurts. "You fucker," I growl, nipping his chin, holding him down. Suddenly I'm straddling his chest, rubbing my cock against his rough cheek. "You said you sucked Wes, right? And you liked it."

"Yes." Rob nuzzles my penis. Then he kisses its head. "I liked it pretty well. Okay, all right, actually I loved it. I sucked him like a mad bastard, to be honest. And now, dude, I'm more than ready to suck you."

"None of this is real. This is all a mad erotic dream," I say.

"Yeah," he murmurs, licking the underside of my shaft. "The last few days have sent me round the bend. I don't know who I am right now. You've been slipping me some kind of mind-altering drug, some kind of aphrodisiac, right?"

"You're the ideal captive, I'd say. The sex-slave I've always dreamed of. Dream or no, I'm going to fuck your face."

I prod Rob's lips with my prick. He angles his head and opens his mouth. When he extends his tongue, gently I place upon it the head of my cock. He takes a deep breath before wrapping his lips around me and taking me tightly in. I look down at him, the fucking paradisial sight of a boy so handsome with my dick in his mouth. He stares up at me, blue eyes glittering crazily. I can name that half-mad shine. It's the hunger of the condemned for clemency, for life. I push my cock into him farther; his tongue flickers along my shaft, and pleasure suffuses me. For long, delicious minutes I ride his face before shifting us onto our sides. I clasp his head, spearing his lips; his new beard brushes my balls and thighs; his forehead bumps my belly's plump curve.

"Not bad for a supposedly straight boy," I say, pumping his mouth till he chokes. "Easy, easy." I pull out till only the cockhead fills his mouth, letting him catch his breath, then thrust down the back of his throat.

"Do you like this? Do I taste good?"

Rob grunts around the mouthful of flesh, nods, and bobs harder. "Hell, already?" I gasp, feeling the rapture cresting, ready to break on his tongue. I pull out, cool down, thrust into him again, and within seconds once more approach climax. "You...said," I pant, gripping his head, "you didn't swallow...but...this time..."

In response, Rob only nods, sucking harder, his cheeks hollowing with the effort. Four more hip-thrusts, five, and I'm shooting my semen into him. He nods again, frantically, sucking so hard it hurts, as I give him a second mouthful. He hums and swallows, keeping his mouth firmly about me.

Done. Simultaneously, the sex-tension leaves us. We go limp, lying there together, my cock growing soft inside his mouth. He sucks me gently now, like a drowsy baby at a breast, and I rub his shoulders. When I finally pull out, a string of post-cum ooze trails behind. I finger it up and rub it across his bearded cheek.

I don't know I'm about to say it till I do. "I promise," I say. Sleepily, I roll us into a ball, his body cupped in mine.

"That tasted pretty damned good. Hell, maybe I'm bi after all." Rob snickers, smacking his lips. "Promise? What do you promise?"

"You're such a fucking gift, Rob. I promise you'll leave here alive. How's that for a reward for good head?" I say it, knowing as I do that once such a thing of deep consequence is announced, it must be honored, no matter what.

Rob gives an audible gulp. "Really? Really, Al? I...really?"

"Yep." I pull him closer and kiss the back of his neck. "I know...well, I'm pretty sure...that your, uh, erotic willingness hasn't been cunningly planned to manipulate me. I do believe that it's been what you said, the fear of dying and the desperation to feel as much as possible before... Though you're taking a risk, you know: the more often I make love to you, the less willing I'll be to let you go. To give up such sweetness."

I clear my throat, then continue. "Whatever the reason you just sucked my cock..." I run my finger over Rob's hip before pulling the covers up over us. "There's no way I'm going to let you die. I was pretty sure before that I'd do anything to prevent that, but now..."

"God, man. Oh, God." Rob sniffles.

"No tears, kid." Beneath the blanket I squeeze his ass. "I'm going to enjoy you as much as I can, and then I'm going to get you out of here. Somehow I'm going to make Jay agree to that. To let you loose before he gets home would be to betray him, but once he's here..."

"Your cum tasted good." Rob sniffles again, his voice rough with suppressed tears.

I laugh. "You've learned to say all the right things, haven't you?"

"No. I'm serious. I—"

"Your cum tastes good too, Rob. How about I suck you off before I fix us breakfast?"

In answer, Rob rolls onto his back. I pull off the blanket; his cock's stiff.

"Yum," I say, looking at his hard-on, then up into his hapless face.

"Al? Will you, uh, do what you did before? My asshole... your greased-up finger, and that spot inside? My prostate? That felt super."

"You bet, kid."

"Al? I want to go home. But when I do—and I'm not shitting you, I swear—I'll miss you. You're one amazing dude."

"To adapt Hemingway," I say, bending down to lick his dickhead and to finger his asshole, "it'd be damned pretty to think so."

chapter twenty-six

"DON'T DRUG ME. Please. I'll be quiet."

Rob's looking desperate again: thin lips set in a pout, forehead creased, eyebrows cocked with concern, blue eyes blinking with panic. I love that look. It's proof of my power, of how much his well being, his comfort, his continued breath all depend on me.

"I can't take any chances," I say. "They'll be right outside. They may come inside."

"I understand. I do. But please don't drug me. I'm afraid I won't wake up."

"Come on, kid. It's almost noon. They'll be here soon."

I tape up Rob's eyes again, then lead him downstairs and into the basement. He keeps pleading as I light a few candles around the room. I push the stool up against the post. I push him down onto the stool. I free him from his bonds only long enough to rub his wrists before I pull his hands behind the post and cuff them together. He keeps pleading as I circle him again and again, using yards of tape to secure his torso and arms to the post till his upper half's immobile. He keeps pleading as I nudge his legs apart, tape his ankles to the back legs of the stool and then, to spare him the pain of tape removal, rope his furry thighs to the stool as well. He grunts with discomfort as I apply all these bonds, and, in between grunts, he keeps pleading.

After breakfast, I called the power people. Some guys are due here within the hour to fix the ice-felled electric line. Problem is, that felled line is not all that far from the house and, knowing the way we locals are, the workmen might want to come in to warm up or use the bathroom. Hell, if I didn't have a hostage here, I'd most likely be inviting them in for coffee. That's just the way we mountain folk are around here. This is the first time I can think of that I regret such compulsive regional sociability.

Right now, Rob's really regretting it too, or, rather, regretting the painful position that the likelihood of visitors has put him in. I've made the tape that binds him very tight. It makes shallow furrows around which the flesh of his chest and arms swells. He wriggles and flexes to no avail. Now I douse a cloth with the soporific we used to take him initially.

Rob can hear the slosh; he can smell its pungent sweetness. "Oh, no. No."

"Relax, kid. It's just a little nap." I lift the doused cloth. "I'm going to put you out, tape your mouth shut just in case, turn the space heater on battery-setting, and leave you here for a few hours. When you wake up, they'll be gone."

Rob shakes his head wildly. "No! Al, oh no, please!"

"Why are you so frightened?" I say, putting down the rag and bottle. I stroke his head; his temples are sweating.

Rob starts sobbing.

"What the fuck?" I say, squeezing his shoulder. "Why are you crying?"

"I just don't want to die. I just don't want to die!"

"You're not going to die. I've promised you."

"The drugs, dude! It's too much like death. Like suffocation." His torso strains against the tape; his thighs bulge; the stool creaks. "Oh, please, no!"

"What is this? Some kind of claustrophobia?"

"Yeah," Rob whimpers. "Kind of. Sort of. I don't know. I'm just... I'm just..."

He's panting now, in a full-on panic attack. When I press my palm to his big chest, it's heaving. Beneath his left pec, his heart's hammering.

"Please *no*, please *no*, please *no*. Oh, God, Al, *please* no."

"Hey. *Hey*." I take his handsome face in my hands and kiss him. "Calm down."

"Or what?" Rob shouts. "You'll beat me again?" He shakes his head and cries harder.

"Shit, kid." I rub his shoulders. "I just can't take any chances. If you're not knocked out, and if they come into the house for any reason, even if you're really gagged tight, they might be able to hear you if you shout."

"I *won't* shout. I won't!" Rob shouts. "I *won't*!"

"You're shouting," I say, patting his cheek.

His mouth twists in a split-second smile. Then he sags. He licks his lips. "Please listen to me. I have something important to say to you."

"Yes. But hurry. We don't have a lot of time."

"You promised me you wouldn't let me die. And I can trust you, right?"

"Yes." I wipe sweat off his face. "I promised you. I stand by that, no matter what. I won't let you die, kid."

"Look, you've known me better than any guy. Hell, any person anywhere, ever. Hell, Al, you've known my body better than Sarah. For whatever reasons, you've...loved me more than anyone, I think. You've taken risks—first to kidnap me, then to be kind to me, then to let me see you—masked, but still—and now you've told me you're going to take the biggest risk, to see me get home safe. Right?"

"Yes."

"So *I'm* promising *you*. I'll sit down here—tape my mouth, shut me up, however you want, just don't drug me—and I'll be so damned quiet that no one—no one!—will know I'm here. You can have those power guys in for a goddamned tea party all afternoon, and I swear, I swear, I won't make a noise. Because I'm pretty sure I don't need them. Right? To save me? Because you're going to save me. This is the risk I'll be running: taking you at your word, not calling for help, believing you'll keep me safe and help me later."

I hold Rob; he collapses against me. Then, without a word, I cap the bottle and toss the drugged rag into the corner. "All right, no drugs." From my pocket, I pull the rubber ball. "Ball and tape instead."

Rob's lips tremble. "Oh, no."

"Hurts your jaw bad, doesn't it?" I ask.

"Y-yeah."

"I could stuff a bandana in your mouth, but Jay would call that coddling, and, well, he's right. 'Man up,' as your generation would say." I push the ball against Rob's clenched lips. "Come on, open up."

"Uh huh." Rob does what he's told. I stuff his mouth full. I muzzle him with tape, four layers circling under his chin and up over his head so that he can't move his jaw. Next I cover his mouth, another four layers of tape plastered over his lips and wrapped around the back of the post. Finally, I plaster tape across his forehead, wrap it around the back of the post, draw it once more across his forehead, then once more around the back of the post. Now his head's thoroughly pinned down.

"That'll hold you. Fuuuuck, you look hot this way!" I stand back, admiring my handiwork. Nothing is visible of Rob's face now but his nose and stubble-brown chin. "'Pretty harsh,' another of your generation's expressions. Can you breathe all right?"

Rob tries to nod. Slightest of vertical movements.

"Can't move your head, huh?" My laugh's low and satisfied.

Rob tries to shake his head. Slightest of horizontal movements.

"Struggle for me. Let's see if you can work that tape loose."

Rob obliges. For a few minutes he flexes, squirms, and strains. He can shift only about two inches in any direction. I watch, stroking my hardening dick through my sweatpants.

"All right. Good. Shout for help."

"Um?"

"You heard me."

Rob shouts as best he can. "UMM! UHHHHHH!" The muffled sound rises and fades. "MMMMMMMMM!" My dick grows even harder.

"Okay, they *might* be able to hear you if they're upstairs, but I doubt it. Moot point, right? Because you're going to keep your promise the way I will mine?"

Another attempt at a nod.

"It's a pact," I say. I pat his taped-up, bound-down face. He breathes hard through his nose, a frightened snuffling. Then I flip on the space heater, blow out the candles, ascend the stairs, and lock the door behind me.

chapter twenty-seven

IT'S STRAIGHT OUT of fucking Edgar Allan Poe's "The Tell-Tale Heart," a casual conversation directly above a hidden crime.

Only one lineman shows up for the job. He's very tall, six foot four, I'd say, several inches taller than me. He's good-looking too, with a bushy honey-blond moustache. After several hours of work and a quick trip back to town to pick up some equipment his assistant forgot to pack, he's fixed the power; the light's are on again.

He's in no hurry. He asks for coffee. We sit at the kitchen table, just a few yards above where Rob waits. Today, the telltale heart is undoubtedly mine, throbbing with suspense, and so it does for a long time. I'm pretending to listen, with the occasional polite "Yeah?" or "Wow," or "Uh huh?" but meanwhile I'm remembering everything Jay's told me about prison—the tiny cells, the shitty food, the endless hours, the bloody rapes in the showers. After about fifteen minutes of this guy's baritone chatter, I begin to grow calm, when the gagged screams I half-expect to erupt from the basement have not materialized.

The guy's name is Jerry. He tells me about the glamorous professional photographs his wife had taken of her for their tenth anniversary. He even shows me a couple on his phone: she's pretty, with curled hair, an overly painted face, in various forms of trollopy undergarments I can never remember the names of. Camisole? Teddy? Negligee? Then he shows me some photos of their last trip to Hawaii. Then he tells me about the time a stray cat nested in his truck engine, and he drove the truck to the Chevrolet garage for some work, and he opened the hood, and the cat jumped out and sank its teeth in his forearm, but he overpowered it and tossed it into a box a mechanic lent him, and he took it home and gradually tamed it, and now it comes whenever his wife calls its name.

Between his time on the power pole and his coffee chat, it's late afternoon when Jerry shakes my hand hard and heads out into the rain. I watch him drive off. I pour another cup of coffee and sip it. Before my eyes, drizzle stipples the kitchen window. Inside my head, Rob's emitting muffled sobs against tight layers of tape. He tries to move his head, tries to shift his torso, fails.

It's called delaying gratification and highlighting power. I start a wood fire, shift from coffee to the Maker's Mark Jay and I save for special occasions, take to the couch, and get cozy under the afghan. I read a chapter of Faulkner. When twilight gathers, I unlock the basement door, flip on the light, and head downstairs.

Rob gives a deep groan as I reach the bottom of the steps, another groan as I stand beside him and study him. He is, of course, unchanged, in the same immobilized position I'd left him. Except, again, the combination of his drool and his struggles have dislodged the gag, just as it did the last time I left him here, so that, instead of completely covering his mouth, the tape's become a wet silver roll threaded between his teeth. The rubber ball in his mouth gleams and drips with spit. When he bites down on it, a thin veil of drool pours over his chin like a waterfall. His chest and belly are saliva-streaked; his pubic hair's bedewed with drops. On the floor below the stool he's bound to is a rank yellow puddle. After so many hours down here, he's pissed himself.

I touch his face. He whimpers; a deep flush covers his chest. "You're so beautiful like this," I say. "So, so beautiful. Like a helpless hero. Do you believe me?"

Another tiny attempt to nod. I stroke his nipples; they harden immediately. I drop my hand to his limp cock and start stroking.

"Do you want out of this?"

"Uhhhhhhhhh! Um umm."

"I'm not going to let you loose until you cum for me. Will you cum for me?"

I spit into my hand and stroke him harder. Already his dick's rising.

"Um hum."

I bend to his chest and nibble his nipples. He jumps, manages another minute nod, and thrusts as best he can into my fist. In about three minutes he shoots. His cum arcs across the room, spattering the concrete floor a good six feet from us.

chapter twenty-eight

THESE ARE MORE contentment-groans Rob's making. Not the groans I've heard before, ones that say, "Why the fuck did you leave me tied up here in the dark for five hours?" or "Oh, God, I'm so embarrassed. I pissed the floor!" or "Please don't beat me any more," or "Please, no, don't, my asshole's still sore." These are groans that say, "Oh, you've made me suffer so much, but now, damn, that feels so good!"

After a few hours of ESPN, several rounds of whiskey sours, and more "redneck food," to use my captive's expression—Vienna sausage sandwiches and mustard greens flavored with bacon grease—Rob's newly showered. He's lying on a towel atop my bed in low lamplight, his cuffed hands stretched above him and tied to the headboard by a short rope, his ankles taped together. That's the extent of his bonds tonight. No blindfold, since I'm masked again. I apply more lotion to his knife-marked chest, then roll him over and do the same to the knife-marks and belt-bruises on his back and ass. When I'm done, I lean back against heaped pillows, pull his head onto my chest, and cover us with blankets. We watch the fire in silence; we share a glass of Maker's Mark.

"You kept your promise," I say, kissing his forehead. "You didn't make one sound. Could you hear us?"

"Yes. I could hear the floor creaking right above me. I could hear your voices for a long time. Mainly his voice, I think."

"Yeah." I grin. "The guy was a talker."

"Why did you leave me down there so long after he left? I could hear him leave. The voices stopped, and I waited a long time for you. That's when I pissed myself. I'm really sorry. I just couldn't hold it any longer. Why didn't you come right down?"

"I was savoring it."

"Savoring what?"

"The situation. Having you still here. Knowing you were down there suffering and powerless. Aching for me to return."

"To lift me from the grave," Rob whispers. "Yeah."

"You kept your promise. I'll keep mine. But that means I have to give you up, give you your life back."

"Yeah. I want to go home. I miss Sarah, airhead that she is. I miss my dad, asshole that he can be. I miss my life. But..."

"But what?"

"You're so warm," Rob says, snuggling closer.

"You too. I love you naked."

"And bound?"

"Yeah." I chuckle. "Perceptive brat. Being able to control your body—whether you can move or see or speak—it's a gift. A beautiful gift. It's a dream come true. Those months watching you, I'd fantasize about having you tied up and in my bed, gagged and in my power."

I run my fingers through his short hair and close my eyes. "For so much of my life I've wanted men I could never have, could never even touch. I used to fantasize about tying them up and abducting them. Because then I could touch them whether they were willing or not. I could keep them. I could make them stay. They'd be unable to leave me."

I open my eyes and kiss the crown of his head. "I wanted all that the first time that Jay...that he pointed you out and I started stalking you. You're so manly. To control such manliness..."

"It gets you hard." Rob nudges his hip against my semi-erect cock.

"Yes."

"Makes you feel powerful."

"Yes."

"Yeah, all us guys like to feel powerful, and, sure, often that's at another's expense. But you're mixing mercy with power. You have from the beginning of my time here. Why?"

"Because...this isn't a fantasy. It's not as easy as that. As much as I'd like the world to be all about me and what I want, it isn't. Stalking you, I fell in love with you, and, having you here, touching you at last, getting to know you, I love you even more. Now you're more than just a sight to soak in, a finely shaped piece of young flesh to handle. You've become more than a tool. I care about...your fate, your wishes. And it would be crazy to kill the thing I love, as—"

"As Oscar Wilde said. Yeah, I know. I told you I liked poetry. If you're in love with me, what about Jay?"

"I love him too. We've been together for a good while, and I'd do just about anything for him. But not..."

"Murdering me?"

"No. I won't let him murder you. As long as you don't see our faces, I'm going to take the chance that, once we release you, you won't be able to track us down."

"Honestly, I'd love to send your guy to prison for what he's done to me, but, even if I could do that—and I doubt I could, since I have no damned idea who you two are or where I am—I don't know if I would."

"And why is that, boy?" I take a last slurp of bourbon, put the empty glass on the bedside table, and hug him to me.

"Because you'd go to prison too. And, after all you've done for me, and all you say you're going to do, I don't want that."

I look down at him, stunned into silence. He gazes up at me, his eyes peaceful, frank.

And the phone rings again. "Fuck it." Rolling over, I snatch it up off the bedside table. "Yes?"

"Howdy, lover, plugged that little pig's ass yet? Hey, been thinking about you. How's the ice?"

Jay. More raucous partying in the background. Bad connection. His voice is bright, nervous, and fast, not slow and slurred with drink.

"Hey, honey. We lost power. It's fixed. I put the captive in the basement. He behaved. The lineman—"

"Hey, you should see this place, babe. Potted ferns and all. Stained glass. I'm going to make lots of money on these deals we've struck. Where's Drake now?"

"He's here with me. Tied. He's given me no trouble at all."

"Where's here?"

"What, Jay?"

"Where's here? In our bed?"

"Well, um, no. The living room."

"Liar. You're a liar." Jay's voice is smooth, cold. "You've got him in our bed. Get that shit-eating little fucker out of there. Put him in the back room. Don't give him any heat."

Dammit. I rarely lie to Jay because he can always tell by my tone of voice when I do. "Jay, we talked about this. You were cool with it. Allowing him blankets." I get up off the bed and start pacing before the fire.

"Fuck it!" he explodes. "You're riding that hot little bitch in our bed? I'll kill him, Al." His voice drops into an oily softness. "I'll gut the cunt."

"I'm *not* fucking him. You *told* me to fuck him!"

"Not fucking him. What are you doing with him then? Snuggling with him? Don't think I haven't noticed the way you look at him. That first fucking day, him knocked out in the van, you peeling his clothes off while I was taping his pretty mouth, you staring at his sweet little athletic body, wanting to eat him up like candy. You used to look at me like that."

"I *still* do, but maybe you're too busy drinking and wheeling and dealing and telling me what to do to notice. Or too busy taking drugs. You're not drunk, Jay. I can tell. Your voice is strange. But it isn't alcohol; it's something else. Are you on something? Did those trashy pricks give you something?"

Jay snickers. "Get that stick out of your ass, Al. You get a hard buzz on every goddamn evening of your life. Don't lecture me about getting high. I'll bet you're drinking right now. And don't call my buds trash. We're all white trash, ain't we? Yeah, I took a little something. Didn't sleep last night. I need to stay up, make some more connections. This isn't about me. This is about you drooling over that boy-cunt."

"The boy's...hot. Sure. You think so too. Isn't that one of the reasons we took him? Because you wanted to get your 'cock up his pretty ass,' to use your words? I guess my ass isn't enough for you anymore."

Jay snorts. "When I get home, next couple of days, I'll *slaughter* him. You've forgotten something, baby. This isn't about how hot he is, but how much *his fucking father* deserves to suffer. We're both going to pound his tight little asshole bloody. We're going to stuff that boy with dick at both ends, and then I'm going to beat his good-looking young face in, and then I'm going to cut his throat and hand you the shovel.

And *his fucking father* can go to his grave wondering what the hell happened to his smart, gym-built, tight-assed, blue-eyed *son*."

I try to keep my voice even. "No. No, Jeff, uh, Jay. You won't."

"No?" His voice drops lower. I can barely hear him above the background noise at his end. "Why is that?"

"Because I won't let you." I stop pacing and lean against the mantelpiece. I swallow, and then I say it again. "I won't let you."

Jay laughs, a sharp-edged sound. "You think so?" he says. Then the phone goes silent.

I close the phone; I turn it off. When I look over, Rob's curled up on the bed staring at me.

"Oh, Jesus," he mutters. "Oh, no."

"How much could you hear?"

"Of what he said? The word 'slaughter' stood out. Something about my father. Is Dad refusing to pay the ransom?"

I'm trembling now, adrenaline kicking in. "No, it's not the ransom." I climb back into bed. "I think Jay's on some kind of damned drug. I've never heard him talk like that." I embrace Rob; he curls back against me. We shiver together.

"Please. Let's just leave. You could take me home now. Before he gets back."

It's a temptation. I think of dealing with Jay face to face—his anger, his apparently drugged state—and I want to run. We've never come to blows before, as hotheaded as we both can be, but the way he was ranting, who knows what will happen when he gets home? Then I remember all the years together, the slow way he came back to himself after that long prison term, the months of therapy, how funny and passionate and caring he can be.

"No. I won't let him hurt you, but I won't abandon him. Besides, the roads are still likely to be icy."

Rob sniffles. He huddles against me.

"Please don't cry, son. You're just going to have to trust me, like I trusted you this afternoon. Thanks to you, I wasn't hauled into custody today. I won't forget that. You're just going to have to believe me when I say that I'll take care of you."

Rob rolls over. "I do believe you." He presses his face into the valley between my pecs and takes a deep breath. "You smell good," he says. "Your chest hair tickles my nose," he says.

"Shhh," I say, rocking him in my arms. "Get some sleep."

"Can't just yet. Too scared. Still hearing his voice. Can we just talk for a while? Can you tell me anything about yourself, Al? I know it's important that I don't know who you are or why you took me, but—"

"Why we took you? The ransom."

"I don't really believe that any more, but whatever. Anyway, you know me so well, I just want to know you some."

"Hmmm. Well, once upon a time..."

Rob rolls his eyes. "Oh, please!" He runs his lips over my chest, then nips my right pec.

"Ouch! What are you doing?" Chuckling, I smack the side of his head. "You'll give Daddy some respect if you know what's good for you. Want another beating?"

"No. It's just that you're rocking me like a little boy, and now you're giving me 'Once upon a time'?"

"All right, smartass. Enough talk from you. It's late." I fetch the tape from the bedside table and rip off a long strip.

"Oh hell, I should have known. Guess I asked for it." Rob gives a bleak grin as I attach one end to the nape of his neck. He doesn't resist, keeping very still as I smoothe tape over his lips, under his ear, and back to his nape, finishing up where I started.

I look down at him, smiling. He looks up at me, a grin faint beneath the silver-gray. I kiss the thin imprint of his lips. "Just fucking breathtaking." He bumps his face against mine—best attempt at returning the kiss he can manage, given his situation. Then he snuggles his head against my chest. "Umm hmm," he says, meaning, I can only imagine, "Go on."

"Once upon a time, there was a chunky kid with glasses in a little mountain town. He read a lot; he didn't have many friends. His Daddy taught him to farm and put up hay, taught him what kind of tree was what. The kid didn't much like people. He was happiest in the forest, down in the glens, among the leaves and ferns and moss. Though that moss wasn't as pretty as this."

I rumple Rob's pubes; he jumps and snickers.

"Then he outgrew the glasses, got good at football. He fell in love with his coach and with several of his teammates. He figured out he was different. He hid it. It was easy to hide. He looked and acted like all the other guys in town. Except his manners were a little better, thanks to his mother, and he was shy. He was big and bulky and hairy real young; all that made him feel awkward, but it was handy for the team and for hiding how he felt. You comfortable?"

"Huh uh." Shaking his head, Rob tugs at his hands, still roped above him.

"Ah, okay. Right." I unknot his hands from the bed but leave them cuffed. "I don't need to chain your neck, do I?"

Rob gives me another vigorous shake of the head.

"You leave that tape on your mouth, okay? It doesn't come off until I take it off. You try anything in the middle of the night, and—"

A third headshake, even more vigorous.

"And the pact's broken. Okay?"

"Mhm huhm." Rob folds his arms under his chin, settles his head on my shoulder, and falls still.

"I'm responsible for you, son. Saint-Exupéry says you become responsible forever for what you have tamed. So, anyway. Then the burly boy grew up; he went to college; he graduated with honors. He slept around, but none of that went real well. He caught crabs a couple of times. Guys would fuck him—he really loved getting it hard up the butt, and sometimes he was ashamed of that, to be so manly but to love getting screwed, 'like a woman,' to use your words—but then those guys would never call him back. Our sad hero lived alone for years. He was more at home in his workplace—he felt needed there—than in his apartment."

I sigh—that lonely life seems very long ago, but it's still no fun remembering it. Wrapping my arms around Rob, I pull him closer. "Till, in a gay bar one night, he met a big guy who looked a lot like him. Deep blue eyes, kind of like yours. Biceps like oak boughs. Hairy pecs like a woodland mountain range. A cock like a hammer, the sex drive of a satyr. This guy stayed. This guy was crazy and charismatic and broken—all the fascinating, mesmerizing ones are damaged to the bone, have you discovered that yet? Well, at any rate, seemed like our sad hero could only feel passionate about charming fuck-ups like that. And this big hot guy loved him. So I—so the sad hero, the burly boy owes the big hot guy a lot, he's got to stay with him, protect him from himself. You asleep yet?"

"Hum mm."

"You ought to be. That's the end of that fairy tale. So far." I begin rocking Rob gently, and I don't stop till the boy's snoring against my chest.

Insomnia. Again. No surprise, after that phone call. This sweaty mask doesn't help. Might as well read on the couch again. I rise, inadvertently waking Rob.

"Hhhm uh!" he protests, cuffed hands reaching for me, fingers clawing the air. "*Hhhh* uh!" Fear contorts his face.

"Okay, okay. Let me turn off the fire and the lamp." I do so, then climb back into bed. He rests his head on my chest; with one arm I hold him; with the other hand I stroke his taped lips, his cheeks and chin, till he's snoring again.

chapter twenty-nine

BAD DREAMS WAKE me. Something about Jay with a club, beating Rob before beginning on me. Then a tornado battering the walls, its sucking funnel descending on the house, the furniture seized up, while I cower beneath the basement stairs, Rob clasped in my arms. Then Jay with a rabid dog's teeth, lips curled back and foaming.

Rob's sound asleep, but when I return from a quick pad to the toilet, he's moaning and jerking too, inside his own nightmare. "Hey, hey." I pull him to me, squeezing a shoulder. With a shout, he sits up.

"Rob, son. Rob," I whisper, "you're all right. No one here but me." For a moment he's rigid, staring around the room. Then he collapses against me.

"Bad dream? Me too. Need to piss?"

Nighttime routine by now, helping him hop down the hall. Back in bed, we lie side by side in the dark. I hold his hands. "All right?"

"Hm uh! Hm uhh!" Shaking his head, Rob rubs his taped mouth against my shoulder. "Mm! Mmmrr!"

"Okay, kid." I begin peeling tape. I'm halfway done when Rob grumbles out of the free corner of his mouth. "Hurts! Beard! Ouch!"

I laugh and keep peeling. "There. Sorry. I'm not shaving your beard, however. You're good-looking without it, but with it you're a fucking knockout. And, to be honest, the sight of your face, that combo of tape and beard and the blue pathos in your eyes...well, damn. So what's so urgent?"

"This." Rob inches down the bed, awkward in his bonds, and to my surprise takes my flaccid cock in his mouth.

"Whoh." I pull away despite myself. "What? Now?"

"I know you're upset and scared after his call. I am too. That's why...we don't have much time." Rob's hand scrabbles at my thigh. He scoots closer and kisses my belly-swell. "I trust you to take care of me. But who knows what'll happen? He's as big as you are. He sounded crazy and angry. He may be on the road right now, driving in this direction, with a head full of chemicals and a gun full of bullets. I don't want to die knowing the only man's dick up my ass was his. Make love to me, Al. Tonight. Keep me bound if you need to, but make love to me...in all the ways I know you've fantasized about for months. Who knows when he'll show up? If anything goes wrong, if... You may be my last lover, the last person on earth I taste and touch."

"Rob, kid, I'll protect you. I swear."

"Listen to me!" Rob shouts. "Anything could happen! I don't want to take a chance. Please!" With that, he cups my balls in one hand and swallows the head of my cock. Pleasure washes up my frame. I groan, clasping the back of his head. I look down, watching this terrified young man bobbing frantically. Hands clenched at that angle, head bowed, he could be praying.

chapter thirty

IT'S AS IF we're passionate and devoted lovers. As if we've shared this old bed for years, intertwining our bodies, rising every morning to make a life side by side. If I could forget all that's happened, only listen to Rob's sighs, cherish his body's excited movements, the way he responds to my touch, I could almost believe he was here willingly. I could almost believe he was determined to stay.

All that's fallacy, the grand subjunctive, As If. But he's here now. And he's not going anywhere for a while. And there's no denying the rapturous groans he's making as I trail my tongue up and down his ass-crack, as I spread his buttocks wide and feast on his tight little hole.

He told me to make love to him in all the ways I've been fantasizing about, and so I am. In the bathroom, I've cleaned him out with the anal spike, and this time he's made no panicked protests. Now he's sprawled across the bed, on his belly, while the fireplace flickers and rain sounds on the tin roof. His hands are cuffed behind him; a bandana's knotted loosely between his teeth, so that he can verbalize without much difficulty in case I get too rough or go too fast. I've propped his loins on pillows, cut his feet free, and splayed wide his legs, giving me easy access to his asshole. His cock, hard and pulsing, is pulled down between his thighs. Every now and then I pull my tongue out of his hole long enough to lap the pink arrowhead of dick-flesh, the long, veiny shaft.

I rim Rob till his fingers are scrabbling air and he's sobbing into the sheets. I heat him up further with a greased forefinger eased up inside him. I work his prostate, knowing the effect I'll get. His sobbing deepens, becoming a bass beast's growl, low in his throat. I stroke his cock and simultaneously work that little convexity inside him till he's half-mad, hips humping the mattress. I want my athletic captive so aroused by the time I enter him that he'll be begging for erotic release.

"Not so straight now?" I say, adding a second finger.

Rob snorts and mumbles. "Nah."

"I'm going to fuck you, boy," I say. "At long last. No one's here to help you. You're bound and gagged; you're completely helpless. Jay's far away. My phone's turned off. You have absolutely no choice but to take my dick up your ass. Right?"

Rob nods, exhaling a long, deep breath. "Yah. Yah."

I pull out, apply more lube, add a third finger, and push into him a couple of inches. Rob winces. I work my fingers around. "Come on, kid. Open up." Slowly his hole expands, accepting me, a wet tightness pulsing around my knuckles.

"Am I hurting you?"

"Nah. Nah." Rob pushes back against my hand; my fingers slip in another inch, then another. He gasps, lifts his head, gasps again, then drops his face onto the bed and lies still.

"You want me to open you up more? I have some dildos." I bend over him, kissing his shoulders, his sweat-beaded temple.

Rob rolls his head to the side. His white teeth gnash the spit-saturated gag. His blue eyes are glazed, dreamy, affectionate. There's no fear in them, no anxiety or resentment. To my immense relief, he seems entirely accepting of his fate. "Nah. Nah. Ah'm ray."

"Ready?"

"Yah."

I've never been harder. I lube my cock up fast. I rub it along his ass-crack, position it against his hole's rosy slipknot, press my groin against his buttocks, and push.

"Ahhhhh UH!" Rob moans, burying his face in the sheets. Very brief resistance, then my cockhead pops inside the circular gate of muscle.

"Huhhhh HUH!" Gasping, Rob shifts the angle of his ass. His body takes me in, inch by slow inch. Within half a minute, I'm lying on top of him, my cock completely inside.

"Oh God," I gasp. The ecstasy of being buried deep within him is even greater than I'd imagined. Addled with ardor, I kiss his shoulders, his head, his cheek, again and again and again. "Oh, kid. Rob, son. I love you. I love you." I must sound insane, but I can't help it. "You're so beautiful; you feel so good. Thank you. Thank you."

Rob lifts his head and gives me another sideways glance. His bandana-muted mouth is curled in a half-grin, but his face is knotted with discomfort. I stroke his head and keep kissing him. Slowly his face relaxes and the look of pain recedes.

"It's not hurting now?"

"Nah. Ga. Gan."

"Deciphering the language of the gagged." I chuckle. "That'd be a fun class to take or teach. 'Go on,' you say?"

Simultaneously Rob nods and squeezes his ass-muscles around the base of my cock.

"Ahmmmm, good boy, sweet answer," I say, commencing that in-and-out rhythm that's every man's root of rapture. In imitation of my favorite porn stars, I give his right butt-cheek, then his left, sharp slaps that make him yelp. "I'm going to fuck your ass in every position I've ever dreamed of. I'm going to fuck you till you're sore and for some time after. That all right with you, Mr. Drake?"

"Uh huh!" Rob pants and bucks.

"And after I shoot a big load inside you, I'm going to suck you off. That all right?"

Rob wiggles his ass against me; his channel constricts once more about me.

"Umm, great! Glad Jay taught you that," I mutter. I press my head to his, wrap my arms around his torso, and begin fucking him harder.

We're existing out of time, it seems. A romantic feeling, an illusion, but still one to savor. I take Rob on his belly for a long time, stopping my thrusts every now and then when pain fills his face, leaving my cock buried inside him, his throbbing flesh wrapped around mine. I pull out at last, only to roll him onto his side. I fuck him in that position even longer, roughing up his nipples with my eager fingers, stroking his long cock.

Every now and then he whimpers with apparent pleasure. Every now and then his erection flags, when the pain comes again. I give us breaks, pulling out, slipping down to suck his nipples and cock before wrapping my arms around him and pushing my hard-on up his ass again. We take a turn bent over the edge of the bed, then once more on our sides.

We finish like this, here: Rob folded beneath me, his knees brushing his ears, his legs over my shoulders, his cock in my fist, my mouth pressed against his gagged lips, our eyes interlocked. "God, boy," I gasp, feeling my bliss mount. "Oh, Rob, sweet boy, I love you, God, you...feel...so..."

That's when Rob's blue eyes grow wider and wilder than I've ever seen them. He shakes and shouts; his calves slide off my shoulders and lock around my waist. "Uh! UH! UHH!" Straining, he pulls me closer; I slide in even deeper.

"Hitting you..."—I pull halfway out, then push in hard—"in the right place, huh? I told...you it can feel great...uhhff... getting...fucked!" I stroke his cock and pound his hole harder. The bed creaks. His head tosses; his thighs tighten till they're shaking. Then he arches his body, bites down on his gag, stares into my eyes, gives a guttural gasp, and cums.

His semen's a serial flood. The first jet rockets across his right cheek; the second spatters his chest; the third covers his belly; the fourth spills over my hand. The inner convulsions of his ass finish me right after. Growling, I give a few last short thrusts, and I spill over, deep inside him.

We stay that way for a full minute, both of us panting, his legs still gripping my waist, my arms propped on either side of his head. Leaning forward, I lick the semen from his cheek and chest. From beneath the tight heat of my mask, sweat seeps down my neck. More sweat drips off my chest onto his, then trickles down his ribs onto the bed. We look into one another's eyes for a long moment before I reach up, tug loose the bandana's hastily made knot, and pull the gag from between his teeth. When I lift my hand to his face, dutifully he laps off his own cum.

"Stay inside. Stay inside me, Al," Rob wheezes, flexing his thighs around me. "Please stay inside."

I nod, catching my breath.

"Well, damn." Rob licks his lips and closes his eyes. "I wanted that. I wanted to know how it felt."

"And how did it feel?" I say. "Did getting fucked make you feel like a woman?"

"Oh, no. Not at all. It hurt at first. The way it did with Jay. But then it felt all right. And then...it hurt some more.

And then it felt great. And then, there at the end—the angle, something changed—and you were hitting me just right up inside. And then it was wonderful."

He looks up at me sleepily and then closes his eyes. "You were right. You did it. You made getting fucked feel great."

"The ultimate pornographic cliché: the rape victim learns to like it."

"That wasn't rape, dude. What Jay did to me was rape. I asked you to, remember?"

"Yes. And I still can't believe it." Soft-cocked by now, I pull out. Rolling over, we snuggle on our sides.

"No wonder you like it up the ass. Especially when a guy's 'sweet spot,' as you call it, gets worked." Rob shifts uncomfortably. "Uh, could you uncuff me? My wrists are really, really sore. The metal..."

I oblige, fetching the key and unlocking the handcuffs. "Oh, ouch!" Rob grunts, slowly shifting his arms in front of him and stretching with a grimace. "Shoulders!"

"Poor kid. I'll fix you up." I massage his wrists and shoulders, then stretch him out and rub lotion into his assorted aches and cuts. But when I pull his hands together to cuff them before him, he shakes his head.

"Don't. Please? Don't you know I'm not going to try to escape? After my silence in the basement? And now tonight?"

I cock an eyebrow. "I know you're scared to death of Jay, and you'd do just about anything to get out of here before he gets back, and I don't blame you. You're really not going to make a run for it?"

"*Naked?* With no money? On icy roads? I don't know where any car keys are. You think I'm going to hit you over the head and bolt? Look, I just want to hold you. Chain my neck up, dude. But leave my hands and feet free. Please?"

"Clever little monster. One by one the shackles fall from you, huh? Like Bacchus kidnapped by the pirates."

"Huh?"

"Don't know your classics? Forget it. Inch by inch, you're closer to freedom. All right." I put the cuffs on the side table and lock the headboard chain around Rob's neck. As soon as we're settled beneath the blankets, he wraps an arm around my waist and throws a leg over mine. Gripping my biceps, he whistles softly. "Damn. Big man. Flex for me."

I do so, blushing with bashful pride. He squeezes the bunched muscle. "Nice. Nice. And this." He runs a palm over my belly swell. "You could be a bodyguard or bouncer."

"Too many hot dogs; too much beer."

"I like your bulk. As I said before, you're no boy. You're ripe, in your manhood's prime. That was one of the things I loved about Wes." He kisses a nipple, then presses his face into my chest hair. "Was screwing me as fine as you thought it'd be?"

"Better. Superlative. Fucking ambrosia."

"Good." He runs his fingers through my belly-fur, tickles my navel, and exhales. "Your cock was inside me, and now your cum's inside me. That was what you wanted?"

"Yes. More than anything. Is your hole sore again?"

"Just a little. I'm a big boy. I'll survive. It gave me more pleasure than pain." Sheepishly, Rob rubs his semen-sticky belly. "So. What now? What happens now?"

"Now that hard rain you hear on the roof thaws the ice. We sleep late tomorrow. Now that the electric oven's working, I make us biscuits and gravy for breakfast. I make love to you as many times as our limited time permits. Jay comes home; we have it out; I rope you up in the van and drive you home."

"How long will that take?"

"A couple of days. Longer if we stop for the night."

"Al." Rob nuzzles me. "Did you really mean what you said earlier? Do you really love me?"

"Yes."

"My father's never said that. I guess he thinks that'd be weak. My mother said it all the time; she loved me a lot. Sarah's said it. But I don't know if I believe her. You... I believe you. But, saying it...that doesn't make you feel vulnerable?"

"Yes, it does. But it helps that I have power over you. For now. And, well, son, as you age, something inside you grows more solid. If you're lucky. So you learn to be honest about how you feel. And not so afraid of consequences. Does that make sense?" I say, massaging Rob's shoulders.

"Yeah, it does. Oh, that feels great," he sighs. "Go on."

"Okay. I learned a long time ago...there was one guy I loved beyond all measure...before I met Jay...that you can't make anyone love you—no matter how wildly and inventively you ravish him, how many fine meals you make him, how many gifts you give him. You love him, he leaves, you learn to live without. So I'm going to love you as hard as I can for the next few days, and then—you're really at risk here, I see that now. I thought I could convince Jay to... Look, he's suffered in ways I can't explain to you, because that knowledge would be dangerous for you...for years, he's used booze to help him forget things, distract him from memories—hell, I have too—but now...you've got to go home. So," I finish, patting his head, "let me hold you for a little longer, and then all this will be over. And I guess you'll have your own set of memories to forget."

"I won't forget you." Rob sounds half-asleep. I can feel the small movement of his lips against my chest. "When I think about how you could have treated me...and how you *have* treated me..."

He rolls onto his back. "I know you don't want to give me up. I know you're sad. Lie on top of me, Al."

"I'll crush you."

"No, you won't. Lie on top of me for just a while."

And so I do. We gaze into one another's eyes for a long time, hands caressing beards, temples, and napes. I rise, just long enough to turn off the fire. When I return to bed, I lay my head on his hard chest and rest an arm across his ridged belly. He strokes my hair; I drift off. The last thing I hear is his unbelievable whisper, "I don't want to forget you."

chapter thirty-one

DELIGHT'S SPREADING THROUGH my torso, a soft teasing that shifts like a butterfly from nipple to nipple. I open my eyes. It's dark and cold in here, but, beneath the blankets, something warm is moving against me, nuzzling and nibbling my chest.

I pull back the covers. Rob lifts his head; the links of his neck-chain clink. "Hey, Al. Awake?"

"Yeah." I rub my eyes. "What are you doing?"

"I'm sucking your nipples." He bends into his announced task: lots of tongue, lip-suction, a little teeth, then some chin-stubble raking the sensitive flesh.

"You want more sex? Oh, damn, the young. Always ready to go again. Ummm. Very nice." I grip his head. "Keep it up."

And so he does. "Rougher," I command. "Hurt 'em a little. Yep, yep, that's right."

"You said this makes you want to get fucked," Rob says, in between tongue-laps and teeth-nips. I hear him spit into his hand; now his wet palm's grasping my hardened prick.

"Ah. I see. This is part of *Carpe diem*, right?"

"Yeah. Would that be possible? To fuck you?" He sounds like a boy asking a girl to dance at a junior high school prom. His hand drops from my cock to my balls and pulls at the sac. "I'm clean, I swear; I get tested every couple of months."

"You really want up my ass?" I bend my knees, drawing up my legs. A finger moves to my taint and runs along the sensitive ridge there.

"Well, I know you like to get fucked, and I've never..." Now he's pulling gently at the hair in my crack, making me groan and shudder.

"Fucked a man's asshole before? For years, no one's fucked me but Jay." I lie back, deliberating, desire shadow-boxing with caution. "If he found out...he'd kill us both."

"I don't want to cause any more trouble than I have," Rob says, taking the tip of a nipple between his teeth and tugging lightly, "but I really want you that way, Al. No way he'd find out. *I* sure wouldn't tell him." He squeezes a buttock and trails a finger up and down my crevice.

"Ohhhh, hell. We really shouldn't."

Rob's finger finds my hole and softly strokes it.

"Well, damn you. Hold on."

I bound from bed, turn on the gas fire, and hurry down the hall. In the bathroom, using the anal spike I'd so recently applied to Rob's hole, I clean myself out. When I return, Rob's on his back jacking himself. His cock's long, nearly eight inches, but relatively slender, meaning that, after years of taking Jay's thick dick up my butt, this one should be easy.

"All clean?" Rob whispers.

"Yep."

"Fuck, you're built. I want inside you."

"Say please." I stand by the bed, fondling my dick.

"Please. Please, Al." Rob winks at me like a coquettish vixen. "Please, Daddy."

"Daddy? Nice!" I can't help but guffaw. Climbing back into bed, I pull him to me. "Suckle Daddy's nips, son, and we'll see what happens. That does tend to flip me into bottom mode fast." I cup the back of his head in my palm and push him down to my chest.

The boy's good, alternating between tender and rough, just the way I relish it. Pretty soon, I'm in the mindset he's hoping for, groaning and bucking. He shifts his mouth to my cock for a few tight sucks, then returns to my chest. Meanwhile, one shy finger is burrowing between my ass cheeks, searching for the less than reluctant opening there, finding it.

"Okay. Yeah. Okay. Your clever plan has worked. I need plowed bad. Here," I say, grabbing lube off the side table, stretching out on my side, and cocking a leg. Within a minute, he's moistened up my crack and is finger-nudging my asshole.

"I'm no virgin," I say, laughing low. "Go on. You won't hurt me."

"Okay." Rob rubs his whiskery cheek against my thigh and pushes steadily. "Wow, you're so hairy back here." Slowly, sweetly, his finger slides in.

"Oh, yeah," I sigh. "Very nice."

"Hot as fire. Damn. And tight. Al, can I... Your sweet spot?"

"Hell, yes. Up a little. Toward the belly, not the back. Yep. Yep! There."

The tickly delight mounts as he works my prostate.

"Does that feel good? I'm not hurting you, am I?"

"Huuhhhh! Does it look like you're hurting me, son?"

"Well, you are grinning pretty wide."

"Uhf, that feels *great*. You're a natural at this. Okay, enough of the fingers," I say. "I want your cock now. Give it to me, son. I want it doggy-style, and I want it hard."

"Ahh, all right." We shift, with a clinking of Rob's chain and a creaking of the bed. I get onto my elbows and knees; Rob kneels behind me, lubing himself up.

"Should we...you want me to use a condom? I'm healthy, I swear to God."

"Bareback me like I've barebacked you. Trust, that's what the pact's composed of, right? I trust you, son. I want your cum inside me. Damn, I need filled up bad."

"I'll go slow, Al. I don't want to hurt you."

"Fuck me *now*, kid. I don't need any more fingers. Push that pretty dick of yours up *in* me."

"Oh, dude, wow. Okay! You bet!" Rob fumbles behind me, applying more chilly lube to my hole. Then there's the blunt head pushing, pushing. I grit my teeth and grunt as a sharp wave of pain shudders through me and just as suddenly is gone. "Ohhhhh," Rob gasps as he slides inside.

I turn my head and gaze up at him. He stares down at me, eyes a blue glitter. His hands grasp my hips. "Great butt," he says. "For a guy. Beefy and broad." He pulls out nearly all the way, then drives in again. "Oh, my God. Oh, my God. So tight. So much tighter...than..."

We grin at one another. "Go ahead, Rob," I say, pushing my rear back against his groin. "I'm fine. It feels wonderful. I love...uhhh! being stuffed full. It's like a...brief completion." I use his trick, squeezing my ass-muscles around him till he moans, his face knotting up. "Give it to me hard. I can take it. Pound me stupid, boy. Plow me raw. Cum inside me." I angle my ass higher and bow my head.

"You got it, Al," Rob whispers, kneading my butt-cheeks before pulling me closer. "Damn, Daddy, you got it."

He starts slowly, cautiously, but within a minute he's spearing me rough and fast. After a time screwing me doggy-style, he rings the changes, moving me through all the positions in which I'd taken him—over the edge of the bed, on my back, on my side—then moving through them yet again. It's when he starts ramming me on my side the second time, his arms wrapped around my chest, fingers squeezing my nipples, his head pressed against mine, that my balls draw up, and before I can even warn him, I'm shouting and thrashing with orgasm, my untouched cock, half-emptied after fucking Rob only hours ago, pumping out a meager load.

"Wow, damn," he gasps, gripping my spasming cock. "Oh, oh, OH!" he grunts in my ear. "Here we go!" His pounding increases in tempo, faster, faster, savage thrusts, and his arms are taut about me, and his hips are slamming my ass, and he's finished, panting hard, sweat filming between his chest and my back.

I grip his spent dick one more time with my inner muscles, making him giggle, before he pops out of me. "Oh, fuck, Al..." I roll over and take him in my arms. He buries his face in my chest hair once more. "Thanks," he breathes. "Oh, thank you! That was fantastic."

Within seconds, Rob's fallen asleep. He snores against me, his breath tickling my torso. I'm too happy, too grateful, for slumber. I hold him, watch the fire leap and the bedroom grow gray with daybreak.

Eventually I rise, turn off the fire, leave him there safely chained to the headboard, and lope downstairs to make coffee and start biscuits. Thanks to the eager impaling my captive's treated me to, my hole is ever so slightly sore, but that minor hurt only makes me smile. It's a sweet memento to match the one I left inside Rob.

Outside, ice is splintering off tree limbs and breaking on the winter-crusted ground; the fog's once more impenetrable. I mix, roll out, and cut the biscuits, then slip them into the oven. When nature's call combines with caffeine and I hit the toilet, I think of Allen Ginsberg, some line about love dripping down the bathroom pipes, as the residue of Rob's lean-hipped humping leaves my body. When I check my phone, I find ten ranting text-messages; it's Jay, of course, wondering why I'm not responding, claiming to be worried about me. No mention of Rob this time; no more threats. Only anxiety, impatience, and a promise to be home day after tomorrow.

chapter thirty-two

THE SAUSAGE GRAVY'S simmering and the biscuits are just about done when Jay calls again. "Where the hell have you been?" he snarls. "Why haven't you been answering me?"

"You sound sober. Good. You were damn nasty last night," I say, stirring the gravy. "So I turned my phone off for a while."

"Ah, baby, ah, I'm *sorry*." Jay's deep voice is slick with charm and regret. "I just was kinda surly on booze, and I got jealous. You know how I get. You used to like when I got all jealous, didn't you? You took it as a compliment. Did you fuck the kid?"

"Yes, I did. It was grand, just like you said." I don't know whether I sound proud or defiant.

"In our bed?"

"No," I lie, making a mental note: wash those damned sheets before Jay gets back.

"Uh huh." Jay sounds unconvinced but doesn't pursue it. "Yeah, that cop-cunt is a cum-dump extraordinaire. Built to be hammered." He chuckles and smacks his lips. "Well, we got more meetings today. Things are thawing here. I'll see you day after tomorrow."

"What kind of business are you doing, Jay? You're not dealing, are you?"

"Oh, God, no." He gives a sharp laugh. "I leave that to Ben."

"Ben's dealing drugs? Oh, great. Are you still planning to hurt Rob when you get home?"

"Ah, naw, baby. I didn't mean that. Ben lent me those pills to keep me up—I was so tired—and I think it made me mean. Meaner than usual. Ha. But you like me mean, don't you, babe? Shoving you down on the bed and riding you till you hurt? Don't you love that? Don't you miss it? It's been too long, ain't it?"

"Yes," I say, taking the thickened gravy off the heat. "Yes, I do love it. Yes, I do miss it." Even as I speak, I know that, if Jay ever found out that Rob's dick had been up my butt—the butt Jay's always regarded as his Top-Man property—there'd be hell to pay.

"I won't damage the kid. I just want to fuck him some more."

"I think we should take him home. I don't think it's good for us to have him here."

"What? Already? After all we've risked to take him? Naw. His son of a bitching father needs to worry and suffer and whine a lot longer!"

"I just want you to promise that—"

"We'll talk about it when I get back. Maybe you're right. Maybe it's time he went away. The kid makes me crazy, I gotta admit. Sometimes all I can think about is raping his tight boy-cunt again; other times I want to cut his throat and watch his last breaths bubble blood."

Before I can protest, Jay coughs hard, then talks faster. "So, I bought you a few surprises, baby. Fancy cheeses and stuff. These big-city markets are full of hoity-toity treats. In return, you gotta give me head. Or maybe I'll bend you over the couch and give you a greasy pokin'. Bet you'd love that, huh? What you gonna make me for dinner when I get home?"

He sounds like his old self: flirtatious, demanding, potty-mouthed, generous. "The stomach and the genitals," I joke. "All most guys care about. Glad I'm a good cook with an eager ass, or I'd have spent my adulthood single. How about barbequed pork chops? With macaroni and cheese?"

"Great! A chess pie'd be nice too. Okay, here's Ben. See you, baby!"

He clicks off. The oven timer beeps. I pull out the biscuits and set the hot cookie sheet on a cooling rack. I taste the gravy; I add pepper. I finish my coffee and watch icicles out the kitchen window drip and break from the eaves. I count the lies I've told since Rob came here. Part of me loves the boy and wants to keep him captive always; part of me wishes we'd never met.

chapter thirty-three

WE EAT BREAKFAST in bed, among sheets soiled with our lovemaking. Rob's famished, slurping coffee, eating four biscuits topped with sausage gravy. I've cuffed his hands in front of him, so I feed him as usual. He smacks his lips, making little humming sounds, opening his mouth wide like a hungry baby bird. Every now and then his blue eyes, glowing with gratitude, meet mine; every now and then his eyes veer to the white blanks dense fog has made of the windows, no doubt imagining the promised return trip home.

"You look pretty happy for a hostage," I say, wiping stray gravy off his chin.

"Happy? Well, this breakfast's tasty. Got to admit, you hill-billies know how to eat."

"My father was a short-order cook in a little mountain diner. He wasn't very good at expressing affection, so he showed his caring in his cooking. I guess I inherited that from him."

"You keep me here much longer, and I'll going to build up a belly like yours. Damned good vittles, isn't that the mountain expression?" Rob smiles.

"Vittles? Well, yeah, we still use that word occasionally."

"Speaking of damned good, so was your ass. Felt as fine as, um, lady-parts. Plus, well, getting fucked with tenderness instead of brutality was a lot better than I expected." Rob flushes, flashing me another big smile.

"I'm happy because you've given me hope, Al. I'm beginning to believe I'm going to survive all this and make it home alive. Everything's thawing; that's a good sign. When do we leave?"

"Jay'll get back day after tomorrow. He called this morning and sounded semi-reasonable. I think he'll let me take you home. Just, for God's sake, don't let him know how comfortable I've made you. And that I let you up my ass."

"I can keep a secret. And speaking of assholes...I need the bathroom."

"Right." I unchain him, lead him to the commode, settle him onto it, and watch him squint with discomfort. "Um," he says. "Ouch."

"Yeah, I know," I say, smiling. "The after-pangs of a good plowing. Was it worth it?"

"For that amazing orgasm you gave me? Yes. But..." He grimaces. Beneath him, toilet water splashes. "There you go. What you left in me." He sounds almost regretful.

"Not the kind of souvenir that stays," I say, wiping him. "I have some work to make up today, now that the computer's operating again. So I'm going to set you up on the couch, okay? And it's time to blindfold you again. This damn mask is making my face itch."

Rob displays the same easy compliance he's shown for days now. Downstairs, I tape his eyes, then his mouth, then his ankles, then, with more tape, secure his sinewy arms to his torso, finally covering him with the afghan. Warmth of another wood fire, melancholy New Age music—we spend the morning like that, I at my desk, he a few feet away, snoozing on the couch.

It's well after two PM when I realize how late it is.

"Hungry?"

Rob starts. He lifts his blinded head and nods.

I rise, only to sit beside him. "You're ready to go home, aren't you?" I stroke his bare chest and the thickening brown of his beard.

Rob nods and grunts. "Umm mm."

"'Too dear for my possessing,'" I sigh.

"Umm?"

"'Thus have I had thee, as a dream doth flatter, / In sleep a king, but waking no such matter.' Don't know your Shakespeare? Speaking of souvenirs...have you read his sonnets?"

Negatory head shake.

"All right. Will you be okay alone for a little while? I'd like to buy you a gift, and I could pick up lunch on the way home. You're comfortable? Warm enough?" I take Rob's hand; he gives me a sleepy nod.

"All right!" I say, excited by my sudden sentimental idea. "I'll be back very soon." I take the precaution of closing up the fireplace, then, grabbing my keys and wallet off the kitchen table, I dash out into the fog.

chapter thirty-four

THE WHITE CAT is sleeping in the front window, as it is almost every time I come by this bookstore. Inside, coffee's brewing and some local ladies are knitting. The Connecticut woman who started this place has made it a real community center. I pat the cat, rub her belly, then head for the poetry section.

This little town is damned lucky to have such a place, and so am I. My reading tastes have gotten so esoteric over the years that I end up having to special-order everything I want, mainly Civil War history. But, as I'd hoped, Shakespeare's in stock. Several of his plays, and yes, a nice paperback edition of the sonnets. Would have liked a handsome leather-bound edition, something fancy, since it's meant to be a Farewell/ Please-Remember-Me gift, but this version will have to do.

Food City next to pick up groceries for Jay's welcome-home meal, and then Sonic, the same place Jay fetched Rob his first meal here. It's only been days, but, after all that's happened, it feels like weeks, months, years. Sonic has new hot dog specials—Chicago, New York, Chili-Cheese, and

All-American—so I get one of each with two orders of sinful tater tots and some sweet iced tea before heading out of the fog-shrouded town and on up the rut-racked road to our remote hideaway.

The cove's nearly opaque with fog, thaw dripping steadily from the spruce. I cut the engine, clamber out with my bags, and am halfway across the muddy lawn when the front door's flung open. My shock's so violent that I drop the bags. What the hell? Have the police caught up with us at last?

I don't have time to contemplate escape routes or worry about the flash of blue uniforms or shouted orders to put my hands in the air. Jay lumbers out onto the columned porch, dragging Rob behind him with a belt looped around his neck. Our hostage is still blinded, gagged, and cuffed, except his feet have been cut free, the layers of silver-gray duct tape I'd left plastered around his torso and arms have been removed, and he's bleeding. Jay's been punching and cutting him, it's clear. The boy's chin is stained a watery red from mixed blood and drool oozing beneath his gag, and a big X has been etched into his chest. The blood flow there is copious, a scarlet scrim veiling Rob's well muscled white; these wounds are clearly deeper than the crosses Jay inflicted before he left.

I understand that X. It means canceled out.

"Hey, bay-by! Where you been?" Jay's voice is a singsong of sarcasm. He's as handsome as ever, thinner somehow after only a few days away. His eyes are burning; his lips lift in a broad smile.

"Jay, what are you doing here? I thought you—"

Rob may be blinded, but at the sound of my voice he starts screaming into his gag, a high, hysterical keening. His cry for help is cut short. Jay jerks the belt about his neck; Rob staggers, releasing a strangled moan.

"You thought I wouldn't be back till day after tomorrow. Yeah, I know. Things change. I convinced the boys to drive us home early. Thought I'd surprise you. Turns out I was the one surprised."

Now Jay jerks the belt again, bending Rob forward.

"Nice juicy hole," Jay says, fingering Rob's ass. "Did you leave a big load here, baby?" Loudly he clears his throat; he spits on Rob's back.

I move a little closer. "Yes. I told you I fucked him. You're acting jealous again. Why? You *told* me to fuck him."

Ah," says Jay, taking Rob's flaccid cock in his hands and giving it a stroke. "But you didn't tell me *he* fucked *you*. This boy-cunt, his cock's all lube-wet and smells like ass. Whose ass could that be?"

Jay shoves Rob between the shoulder blades. Sightlessly, Rob stumbles forward, down the steps. He misses the last one. Tripping, he slams a knee into the snow-and-mud-streaked ground, rolls onto his side in a puddle, and lies there heaving.

"After all these years of being faithful to me, you had to have this pig's cock up inside you? Barebacked, from what I can tell. Took that chance. After all I told you about Zac dying. Months watching him shrivel up like a motherfucking earthworm in the sun. You promised me your ass was mine. Goddamn you both."

Jay strides down the steps. He scratches his head hard; then he spits in Rob's face and kicks him in the crotch. Rob screams and thrashes.

I'm on Jay before I know what I'm doing. I tackle him around the waist and we both hit the ground. "What the fuck?" he rages. "Whose fucking side are you on?!" Without hesitation, he punches me in the right eye. I fall back, growling. Then I lunge forward and swing. My fist crashes into Jay's jaw. He staggers, laughs, spits blood, and returns the favor, the arc of his fist connecting with the side of my head. I hit the lawn hard; mud smears my tongue; for a few seconds, my vision's a black pool spotted with purple water lilies.

I get to my knees, stunned and swaying. Jay seizes the belt still noosed around Rob's neck and hauls him upright. One arm wrapped around him, from his pocket he pulls the knife, the beautiful black blade with the glittering silver edges, the one I myself held to Rob's throat only days ago. "You were right, Al. I don't think it's good for us to keep him here. So he's going into the woods with me. No need for you to watch. I'll be right back."

Unsteadily I rise to my feet and take a step forward. "You're on something again. It's making you crazy. Come on, Jay, this isn't you. You're a ferocious guy, but you're not—"

"Ah, ah, no, Al, no." Jay runs the flat of the knife across Rob's neck. "Get back." Rob's shaking his head and whimpering the same stifled syllable, a word that can only be "Please." I stop, only feet away, fists clenched at my sides.

"I saw the sheets, lover. You all had a grand old time in our bed. He rode you like a whore, and I'll bet you loved it. And there the pretty boy was, all cuddly and comfortable on the couch, your own sweet sex-slave in your own mountain love-nest, and the kitchen cozy and domestic, a regular Martha Stewart scene, with the smell of fresh biscuits. Ever since this *cunt* came here, I've been, uh, less than balanced, I admit, and remembering things I've tried to forget, reasons to hate, reasons to hate, and you've become a liar. And a doting fool. Love and hate, that's us. He was a mighty sweet piece of ass, but that's proven...troublesome. So now I'm going to cut his throat."

Jay tousles Rob's hair; Rob's taped pleading mounts.

"Then I'm going to hack him up and hide the parts in that swamp down the hill. Ground's froze too hard to bury him here. And you're gonna help me. Messy work, but necessary."

Jay gives Rob a one-armed hug, as if they were frat buddies. "Then he'll be gone, and our little caper will be done, and we can get back to the way we were before. This evening we'll break out those fancy cheeses I brought you, and you can cook me that nice meal you promised. Help me now. And I'll forgive you. And everything will be put right, and I will have had my justice, and all those memories—these, and all the ones before"—Jay squints, rubs his head, and shakes it—"we can drown them all. With him."

Rob starts sobbing. He slumps against Jay, then slips from Jay's grasp and falls to his knees, all hope fled. He bows his head and cries like a child.

"Jay." I step forward.

"Al, you motherfucker, you dick-starved slut, you come any closer, I'm cutting your throat after I'm done with him." Beneath Jay's dense black eyebrows, his eyes flash like hot gas fires. He brandishes the black blade, lips curled in a snarl.

"You're going to cut my throat. Me? The man who's stood beside you for all these years? Who's catered to you and loved you and obeyed you even when you were making a fucking fool of yourself, taking wild risks, acting bat-shit crazy. You're going to cut my throat?"

"I will, baby. Don't test me."

"You're high as hell on something. Listen to yourself. Why, after all these years of boozing it up with me, do you suddenly start sniffing or snorting or gulping whatever the hell your trashy buddies have offered you?"

"Why? This," Jay says, giving Rob another fraternal hug. "Having him here doesn't help me forget; it makes me remember."

"So let me take him home. He can't identify us."

"Fuck, no. Why take that chance? Let's gut the bastard."

"And you think you can do that and then live with knowing what you've done? I can't love a man like that. This kid hasn't done anything to us. Jay, if you hurt him, I'll leave you."

Jay licks his lips. He musters a thin grin. "What?"

"You heard me. We've been together for years, but if you don't let me take this kid home unharmed, if you murder him, I'll pack a bag and leave today."

Jay blinks. "Naw. Naw."

Rob lifts his head toward my voice; he pauses in his tears.

"Naw. You wouldn't. You're shitting me. Not after all this time. You can't live without me. I can't live"—Jay grits his teeth—"without you."

For a long silent moment we stand in the fog, the knife still in Jay's hand. My partner and I glare at one another. The muscles in my calves are shaking; I'm tensed, ready to tackle him again if he aims to use the knife. There are no sounds but Rob's deep breathing, the caw of a crow, and water dripping off the porch eaves.

Jay guffaws, so abruptly I jump. He throws back his head and lets loose a belly-laugh. He pats the top of Rob's head with the knife, then pushes him face-first into the snow. "You stay there, shithead," he says, resting a boot on the back of Rob's head. "Okay?"

Rob squeaks. I can see his spastic shuddering from here.

Jay steps forward. He sheathes the knife and then he hugs me. I stand there stupidly for a second before wrapping my arms around him.

"For fuck's sake. For fuck's sake. For fuck's sake," Jay mumbles. "My big old bear, my bottom bitch. Am I dick-whipped or what?"

He hugs me till my spine creaks. Then he pulls back, looks me in the eyes, and punches me in the belly. I drop to my knees, gasping.

"You hungry-assed whore. You win. I'm going over to Ben's for a beer. You have an hour to get that cunt out of here. Be gone then, or I might change my mind. I might be here when you get back, or I might not. So you're *sure* he doesn't know anything that..."

"I'm sure," I wheeze. "I don't want to go to prison either."

Jay stands in the yard glaring as I right myself and then pull Rob's muddied, bloodied body up from the snow-slush. Rob leans on me, and together we limp across the yard and into the house.

chapter thirty-five

I COULD BE packing the van for a down-home picnic: a cooler of pimiento cheese sandwiches, baloney sandwiches, bags of potato chips and fried pork skins, a few cans of Vienna sausages, bottles of water and sweet iced tea. The damn Sonic dogs ended up crushed in the mud during my tussle with Jay, though I did manage to retrieve the book of sonnets, which I've hidden in the van's glove compartment. The Food City groceries I've lugged inside the house and put in the fridge and freezer. Maybe I'll make that celebratory meal when I return, to mark the end of this nasty mess. Maybe Jay and I can salvage one another and find some kind of forgiveness.

Rob's curled up in the back of the van, between unzipped sleeping bags on a blow-up mattress. I've hurriedly cleaned him up, medicated his fist-split lips and bandaged his chest, and, to insure his warmth, dressed him in a black zip-up hoodie, a pair of gray sweat pants, and a pair of gym socks. The usual tape's over his eyes and mouth; his knees are bent, his legs drawn up before him, cuffed hands tethered by a short rope to taped ankles. It's a less rigorous version of a traditional hogtie, more comfortable but equally inescapable. At this point, as hopeful, grateful, and acquiescent as he is, binding him is probably not necessary, but there's no need to take chances, and, besides, I might as well savor my power over him while I can. We'll be parting and he'll be freed soon enough.

By the time I'm ready to leave, Rob's begun trembling and panting, as if suffering another panic attack. He's clearly terrified, afraid that Jay might return before we leave, and eager for our imminent departure, when all his fears will transmute into welling relief.

"Easy, kid," I say, wiping sweat-wet from his forehead. "We're all packed. No need for that knockout drug, right? You're going to be real quiet back here, be a good boy until I get you home?"

"*Uh huh, uh huh, uh huh.*"

I lock the rear doors of the van, climb into the front seat, and slip the key into the ignition. "Ready?" I ask, looking back at him curled up in the dimness.

"UMM!" Rob's head bobs crazily.

"That's gagged-hostage talk for, 'Hell, yes! Let's get the fuck outta here,' huh?" I turn the key; the engine snarls and hums; we're off.

Jay's waiting in his truck at the bottom of the holler as I bounce the van off the dirt road and onto the pavement leading toward town. I wave. He gives me a tight-lipped smile and a military salute. I watch him in my rear-view mirror, half-expecting him to follow, but instead he steers onto the road I just descended and disappears into the woods.

I drive for hours. The fog relents as we reach the interstate. I play country music: Tim McGraw, Brad Paisley, Toby Keith, the Zac Brown Band. Around us, winter-bare mountains loom. Behind me, Rob's utterly quiet, except for occasional grunting and shuffling as he shifts his position from his left side to his right, then back again. I skip lunch, wanting to put as many miles as possible between us and Jay's unpredictability.

It's early twilight by the time I pull into a rest stop along the West Virginia turnpike. I park as far from other cars as possible, but there aren't many to speak of, the evening being as bleak and cold as it is. The mountains are slate-gray about us; somewhere nearby a noisy creek gurgles over stones.

I climb behind the seat, slip beneath the sleeping bag, and nestle against Rob. "Okay, boy, you're hungry, right?"

"Uhm um."

"First we need to have a talk." I slip the hood off his head and peel the tape off his mouth; as usual, he whines.

"Ouch. Damn beard. And busted mouth." Rob licks his swollen lips. "Yeah, I'm starving. Where are we?"

"About an hour from a little roadside eatery I like, the Red Line Diner. I know this route real well, since I drove it a lot back when I was watching you. Since our hot dogs today were ruined, I thought I'd treat you to some great dogs and fries from this diner. Are your wounds hurting you?"

"Not too bad, dude. Thanks for tending them. I—"

Voices passing outside. I clamp my hand over Rob's mouth. "Shush now." He nods beneath my palm. I hold it there till the noise fades.

"So, back to the pact." I lift my hand from his mouth only to caress his beard. "Just so we're clear. I'm taking you home, so you don't want to get me into trouble, right? You could start shouting for help at some point—when I get us meals, when I gas up the van—and that way you'd end up free and Jay and I would end up in custody. Or—"

"Or I could just lie here and not make a sound, like I did in your basement...and I'd end up safely at home...and you'd end up safely at home. Yeah, dude. I get it. Works for me. Okay. I promise. We're still swapping risks."

"No risks left for you, son," I say, kissing the back of his neck. "You're safe with me. For you, the danger's past. I know little back roads where I can park this van for the night, where no one'll mess with us. During the day, you're gonna lie back here, all trussed up and bored out of your mind, listening to my country music..."

Rob makes a face. "Ack. How about some heavy metal?"

I make a face. "Ack. No. And during the night, I'm going to hold you and make love to you. And day after tomorrow," I say, gripping his cuffed wrists, "you'll be free."

"And we say goodbye. For good."

"Yes. If I'm right, you won't be able to find us. And we'll leave you alone. We'll never trouble you again. I swear. It'll be over for you."

"I doubt that. I doubt I'll ever escape it. His cruelty. Your kindness."

"Scarred. Yeah." I pat his bandaged chest. "I know."

"So you and I, we'll never see one another again. And I'll go back to Sarah as if nothing happened. And you'll go back to Jay as if nothing happened." Rob gives a low laugh. "Unimaginable."

His belly rumbles. "Let's go, dude. Let's get to those dogs."

"Ravenous brute. More trouble than you're worth. Does this tape hurt your split lips? Would a bandana be easier on you?"

"You really need to keep me gagged? I swear I'll keep quiet."

"I really need to keep you gagged, kid."

"Kind of figured. Part of that power trip that gets you stiff, right? Tape's fine."

"Good boy." I press a fresh strip of tape over Rob's mouth, make sure he's well tucked in, then drive back onto the turnpike.

Black hills, clusters of lights, the white lines of I-64. Cabin Creek, then the shimmering black flow of the Kanawha River, then Marmet, Charleston, Dunbar, Institute, Cross Lanes. Within an hour, I'm pulling into the parking lot of the Red Line Diner. "Keep quiet," I say before getting out. "The pact, remember. You don't want to be drugged."

The diner's brightly lit, with booths composed of chrome and fake leather, a dull crimson, and walls covered with Marilyn Monroe and James Dean posters. It's full of factory workers tucking into burgers and fries, pinto beans and cornbread—a place I'd normally be entirely content in. But tonight, for obvious reasons, I'm anxious and impatient. The waitress is short, blonde, and exceedingly friendly, but the take-out order takes much longer than I'd hoped. When it appears, I pay, fingers suddenly clumsy and fumbling, then dash to the van with my fragrant haul. The rain's started again; across the road, the Kanawha River streams blackly, reflecting the factory lights on the opposite bank.

I've barely gotten inside and locked the door when there's a rapping on the driver's-side window. "Oh, fuck!" I whisper, dropping the bag of food between the seats. "Not a word, boy."

"Huh um," Rob mumbles.

There's a stranger standing there in the drizzle. He's pudgy, with a bald head and a grizzled face. The rain's darkening the shoulders of his army jacket. I should just ignore him and drive away, but automatic politeness and Rob's previous track record for good behavior both cause me to roll the window down.

"Howdy, buddy," he says. He smells of whiskey.

"Evening, bud," I reply, forcing a smile. We mountain men are always calling one another "buddy," even total strangers. "What's up? What you need?"

"Just wanted to say, 'Go Mountaineers!'" He smiles blankly and sways.

"What?" I grasp the steering wheel, and a fine shaking runs over my hand.

"The 'Eers, man, the 'Eers! You got the bumper sticker!"

For fuck's sake. He's talking about the West Virginia University Mountaineers sticker on the van's back bumper.

"Uh, yep! Big fan."

"Did you graduate from there? I did! Class of '81. Wood Science. The 'Eers sure had a good season, didn't they? Did you go to the Gator Bowl?" He pats the side of the van. "Say, could you do me a favor? My truck won't start. You got any jumper cables in that van anywhere?"

Behind me, Rob emits the slightest snicker.

"Uh, no, bud, no. Sorry. But I'll bet somebody else in the diner might. Lots of folks to choose from." I gesture toward the multitude of huge pickup trucks parked around us. "The place is packed tonight."

"Yeah, sure, okay, have a good evening, buddy, sorry to bother you." He pats the van again, then shuffles toward the yellow lights of the diner. As soon as I roll up the window, Rob starts giggling. "Shut up, brat," I say, annoyed, amused, and relieved all at once. Starting up the engine, I peel out.

A few miles down the road, I find a big Wal-Mart parking lot where we won't be disturbed while we eat. I remove the short rope binding Rob's cuffed hands to his taped ankles. He stretches, grunting first with discomfort, then with relief. As soon as I pull the tape off his mouth, he starts laughing.

"Did you shit yourself?" he asks, grinning blindly at me.

"Pretty much, smartass," I growl. "And you get the Golden Globe for Best Captive Ever."

"The pact, the pact," Rob says. "I owe you; you owe me. And I guess you get the award for Best Captor Ever, if those hot dogs taste anywhere near as good as they smell. Let's eat them while they're still warm!" He opens his mouth wide, the baby bird imitation again. For the next ten minutes, we're leaning against the side of the van, too busy eating to talk, chomping up ketchup-smeared fries and messy hot dogs topped with chili, mustard, and cole slaw. Then Rob's gagged, hogtied, and tucked in again, and we're speeding west toward his native ground, where soon I'll leave him behind and he'll resume his life without me.

chapter thirty-six

I DRIVE TILL my eyes are tired, till the back-and-forth of the windshield wipers becomes dangerously hypnotic and we're an hour into the low hills of eastern Kentucky. Leaving the interstate, I steer us a few miles down a narrow country road, finally pulling the van over into a thicket I've scoped out before. We won't be bothered here.

Rob's silent except for a grunt or wince as I release him from his hogtie, peel the tape off his mouth, and tend to his injured lips and chest. It's very cold in the van, our breaths making clouds, so I shuck off my jacket and ball cap but otherwise stay fully clothed, slipping beside him between the sleeping bags. His head resting on my shoulder, my left arm around him, we lie there listening to the rain, heat building up between us.

"Al? You warm yet?"

"Yeah. You?"

"Yeah. Warm enough to allow a little skin to skin?"

"I kidnap you and violate you and you're asking for skin to skin?"

"Bi-curious, dude." Rob sniggers. "And, as I've said before, you didn't violate me. I asked you to fuck me, remember? It's just that...you know how to use your body to make my body feel good, and it's going to be goodbye soon, so...I just want to feel the heat of your skin, so..."

Rob trails off, his tone sheepish.

"Goodbye soon, yes. Shirtless cuddling, yes." Gratefully, I pull off my sweatshirt and thermal undershirt. Then I unzip the front of his hoodie, uncuff him long enough to strip him to the waist, then lock the metal around his wrists again. Shivering, I adjust the coverings about us. We lie together again, this time bare-chested, snuggled close, my hairy torso to his smooth back. Rain's a soothing sound upon the roof. The slightest of light through the van's windows falls upon us.

"Yeah, thanks. This is nice. I love the sound of the rain," Rob says, his voice a wistful baritone. "Al, who was Zac? The guy who died? 'Shriveled up like an earthworm,' Jay said. He mentioned Zac just before he kicked me in the balls. Which still ache, by the way."

"Sorry about that. I'm aching all over too. Jay used to run with some boxers, so he's got a pretty serious set of fists. Zac was a friend of Jay's. Died of AIDS. Long, slow, painful death. Along with Jay's possessive streak, Zac's one of the reasons that he's always insisted on monogamy and one of the reasons he went so crazy when he figured out that you'd been up my ass. That's all you need to know."

"Wow. Damn. Okay. I swear I'm free of disease, Al; I would never have barebacked you if—"

"Same here, kid. I trust you; you trust me. Speaking of Jay, please tell me what happened when he got home before I did. Did he—?" I pat Rob's butt.

"Violate me, to use your phrase? No. Almost." Rob gives a sharp shudder and cuddles closer. "Well, he was clearly pissed off to find me on the couch rather than in my cold room. He kicked me onto the floor, and that's when he punched me in the face the first time. Then he cut my feet free and dragged me upstairs, bent me over something soft—your bed, I guess—and I could hear him spit into his hand. He said he was going to fuck me till I bled. Then he pushed a couple fingers up in me, and I guess that's when he found out that I was, uh, still a little greased up from before. He must have thought that was funny, because he started laughing. But then he grabbed my dick and figured out that..."

"You'd been inside me?"

"Yeah. So, he...punched me in the face again and that's when he held me down and cut my chest. It hurt like hell, but he said..."

"Let me guess. If you didn't keep quiet, he'd cut your throat instead."

Rob takes a long breath, holds it, and exhales.

"God, kid. I'm so sorry. I shouldn't have left you alone. We never should have, I never should have..."

"Never should have let me fuck you? Maybe. Maybe not. I sure enjoyed it, though the consequences were a lot more severe than I would have imagined. Some pieces of ass you've got to pay a high price for, right?"

"Ha. Yep. That's for damn sure."

"Will I be scarred, Al?"

I trail a hand over his bandaged chest and softly squeeze a pec. "Those are pretty deep cuts. I'm afraid so."

"Scarred and tattooed." Rob sounds almost proud. "Like some kind of ancient warrior. Well, scarred up is a hell of a lot better than dead."

"You never told me about your tattoos," I say, running a finger along the black flames covering his back. It's so dark I can barely make them out.

"Started as a cover-up. My buddies warned me not to get my girlfriend's name inked on my back, but I didn't listen. She and I broke up about six weeks after I got that tattoo. So...I opted for black flames. I'm a Leo—sun and fire and all that. Seemed cool at the time. Now they remind me of my mother. She was cremated."

Rob sighs. "Mom really loved me. Sometimes I don't think my father ever did. I loved it when she scratched my back. Sarah acts like it's a big imposition if I ask."

"Are you asking me?"

"Yeah. I guess." Rob's voice is almost inaudible.

"So sheepish; downright adorable. I'll take any excuse to touch you, son. Roll onto your belly."

I scratch his broad shoulder blades, the knobby ladder of his spine. Rob sighs again, contentedly.

"Is that all right? After I beat you here—"

"No, don't stop. It feels great."

The back-scratch moves into massage. "Oh. Oh, yeah. Uff. That's super," my captive groans as I work the tight muscles of his neck and shoulders. Hands tired, I cease my efforts, stretching out on top of him.

"Al? Dude?"

"Can't breathe? I know I'm heavy."

"Naw, dude. I, uh, would you blow me?"

I slide off Rob, roll him over, and tug his sweatpants down to his thighs. His cock's fully erect. Straddling his chest, I unzip, pull out my own cock, and bump his bearded cheek with it. "You first. Dude."

chapter thirty-seven

MY HOSTAGE AND I take turns: hips humping mouths, beards bedewed with cum, throats pumped full of juice. I fold him in my arms; we sleep as closely as two men can.

Morning is Bob Evans, coffee and sausage biscuits to go. All day, Rob remains the ideal prisoner. Curled up behind me on his mattress, he makes no muted protest, no muffled complaint, and, rather than trying to summon help when I pull into a service station to fetch gas, he keeps absolutely silent. When necessary, I drive us down back roads, free his feet, and lead him into stands of trees for hurried bathroom breaks. The rain continues; the hills disappear. We move into the Midwestern plains: long straight interstates, big gray skies, acres and acres of stubbly cornfields, old snow lying here and there between the rows. Boring landscape to hillfolk like me. I run through more country CD's; I park in the next rest stop for a lunch break; we split pimiento cheese sandwiches from the cooler, a can of Vienna sausages, a bottle of sweet iced tea. Rob heaves a sigh in between bites. "I'm sure going to miss your white-trash cooking. All Sarah and I eat is fast food." Afterwards, I curl up around my hogtied boy and we nap together for an hour. Then another tape-gag and we're back on the road.

A light snow starts falling at dusk, scuttling like white snakes in the wake of passing cars. Dinner's the baloney sandwiches and barbeque pork skins I packed, in another rest stop. I drive till ten PM, then pull off the interstate into one of the sheltered spots I know. It's a little grove of pines near a pond, the snow-dusted evergreen boughs providing a nice shield against the prying eyes of anyone who might wonder about a big gray van parked in the middle of nowhere. We're mere hours from getting Rob home; I'm not about to be caught now.

I double-check the locks and climb into the back. Rob's shivering on his side. Without words, I slide in behind him. We lie like that for a long time; I hold him close and stroke his tape-swathed face. He moans feebly and nestles against me.

Now I pull the tape off his mouth. He licks his lips. "Al, could I have some water? The salt in those pork skins dried me out." I share sips of bottled water with him before undoing the tether between his wrists and ankles and settling us into bed again. We lie on our backs, sides pressed together from shoulders to calves.

"Last night," I say.

"Yeah," he replies, stretching his long-restricted limbs with a low moan. "Tomorrow night I'll be sleeping in my own bed. And you'll be far away."

"As far as I can get. What are you going to tell the cops?"

"What can I tell them, dude? I was drugged, abducted by two big guys whose faces I never saw, spent days bound and gagged in some place in the country several days' drive from where I was taken. I was beaten and cut."

"And raped?"

Rob snorts. "I'm not going to tell them *that*. Can you imagine how people would look at me if they knew? Fuck, no. Anyway, other than that I'll tell them the truth. That the ransom never came, but one of the kidnappers relented and brought me home. There never was a ransom request, was there? You two took me for other reasons."

"No comment."

"And you? What's going to happen with you and Jay? I heard you all come to blows. I heard him punch you."

"He's never struck me before. I don't know what'll happen. Hell, I don't even know if he'll be there when I get back. He may leave me."

Rob rolls over, feels for me, then slips his cuffed hands over my head and hugs me.

"Fuck," I say. "He may leave me. Sometimes I'm so glad we took you, and sometimes..."

"I feel the same. Talk about frigging ambivalence. Both our lives are screwed up. Hey, uh, Al, can we get naked? Last night and all..."

A few minutes of fumbling rearrangements, and Rob's cuffed arms are draped about my neck again, his bare body squeezed against mine.

Al?"

"Yep?"

"So are you going to make love to me one last time?"

"Yes. Absolutely. Not now. I'm so tired. Driving all day... Not as young as I used to be."

"Al? Do it rough. I want to feel you after you leave me. For a little while. I want your body to linger in my body. On my skin."

I chuckle. "Boy, that's one request I'd be delighted to fulfill. Let's take a little nap, and then..."

I close my eyes, exhaustion swamping my frame, my captive's arms about my neck, his fingers combing my unkempt hair.

chapter thirty-eight

ROB'S MOUTH WAKES me. I find him huddled about my waist, sucking my cock. "Just lie back," Rob mumbles around my flesh. "Just lie back and let me make you feel good, okay?"

I obey. I hold his bobbing head in my hands, close my eyes, and savor the feeling, the bliss of this beautiful boy lapping and pleasuring my body. Rob cups and tugs on my balls, gently rakes my cockhead with his teeth, and deep-throats me with choking eagerness. I'm only a minute or two this side of climax, hissing through gritted teeth, moaning, "Boy, boy..." when his mouth releases me with a pop. He gets onto his knees beside me, drops onto his elbows as if he were prostrating himself before a king, and props his bruised ass in the air.

"Go ahead, dude. Go ahead," he whispers, head bowed. "Ride me, dude. Ride me."

We're in no hurry. We have all night. I eat his ass long and tirelessly before lubing us up and prodding my cockhead against his hole. I enter him slowly, an inch at a time. Even after such a lengthy rimming, his ass-knot is still tight. When I'm halfway in, he flinches, lifts his head, and gasps, "Oh! *Oh*! Al! Oh, it hurts! Oh, please! Oh, easy!"

"Want me to stop, boy?"

Rob hangs his head and shifts the angle of his butt. "No, uh! No! Just go slower. Uhm. Easy. Okay. It's better now. I'm ready. Give it to me. I want to hurt tomorrow. To remember this. Fuck me, Al, please."

I give him a few short strokes, then push all the way in and start ramming the boy hard. Wrapping my arms around his chest, I torment his stiff nipples, pinching and tugging, digging into his pecs with my fingernails. He whimpers and sobs, head tossing, and still I ram him.

"Damn you," I pant between clenched teeth, slamming in and out. "You've fucking ruined my life. How the hell am I... uhmm, yeah, I love how you grip me like that...from inside... how the hell am I going to forget this?"

"Damn you too," he whines. "Oh, it hurts! Fuck! No, no. God, *don't* pull out! Keep going! How am I going to...oh, man, yeah...forget any...ohh!...of this either? Uh uhh!"

I pull out only long enough to shove him onto his belly before roughly entering him again. I clamp a hand over his mouth and hammer his hole with sweaty violence, till Rob's drooling and squealing against my hand. Then I roll us onto our sides and grip his cock, which is hard and oozing precum.

"Hitting your spot, boy?" I push in deep, shift my hips, and punch his hot depths with my cockhead. "Feeling good?" I bite his shoulders, his neck, his ear. I stroke his drooling dick, tight and fast.

"Yes! God, yes!" Rob shouts against my stifling hand. He writhes against me, his ass meeting my cock with answering thrusts of its own.

"Damn you, boy. Goddamn you. I love you, boy. I love you," I growl, unable to help myself, a pathetic chant on the eve of parting. "Fuck, fuck, *fuck*, I don't want to give you up."

"Oh! Oh!" Rob yells. "Al! Oh, hell!" He cums, four spurts, into the blankets, into my hand. As before, the orgasmic pulsing of his asshole finishes me immediately thereafter, and soon we're slumped limply together, shivering and panting like worn-out long-distance runners. I lick Rob's cum from my hand and kiss him, smearing his lips with his own juice.

We cuddle and drowse. In a bit, we rise, pissing in the same coffee can. Outside, a fine snow continues to sift down, covering the hood of the van. Then we're spooning again beneath the covers. I hold Rob while he sleeps, listening to his mumbles, sighs, and snores, and wonder where I will be sleeping tomorrow, what I'll find when I get home.

chapter thirty-nine

I WATCH THE dawn's slow seep, and I watch Rob sleep. The windows of the van are coated with snow, creating a kind of cocoon, muting the light, as if we were still back in the cove, encapsulated inside its wintry pearl of fog. It's completely silent here, except for the cheep of birds somewhere out in the pines.

I pull back the covers, despite the deep chill, prop myself on one elbow, and look over Rob's nakedness for the last time: the snowy skin, the bloodstained bandages, the bruises and tattoos. Time to say goodbye. I finger his nipples, swollen from my violent attentions. I stroke the curves of his pecs, the ridges of his belly, the sinewy lines of his arms, the flaccid length of his dick, his curly pubic hair. When I nudge him, he rolls over, muttering in dream, and I play with the hair in the crack of his ass, I run my tongue over his tattoos. "Al?" he sighs. "Is it morning?"

"Shhh," I say, beard-nuzzling his back. "Onto your belly. Just keep quiet and keep still."

My heart's pounding; my throat's tight; my head's swimming. I cover him with panicked kisses. His head, the nape of his neck, his shoulder blades, his spine, his buttocks, his thighs, his calves, and the soles of his feet. He lies beneath me, complaisant, heaving sighs. "Roll over," I order, nibbling a toe. When he does, I continue: deep kisses upon his brow, his nose, his cheeks, his mouth, his pecs and nipples, his belly, the tip of his cock, his thighs, his feet. I finish with an arm around his waist, a finger up his ass, and his cock down my throat. He grips my head with cuffed hands, whimpering and thrusting, and soon he's cum again, a final load filling me. I hold his semen in my mouth, savoring it, before regretfully swallowing. His taste lingers faintly on my tongue.

I sit up and put my face in my hands, thankful for the tape over Rob's eyes. Sobs are gathering in my gullet. One slips out; the rest I choke back.

"Al? Dude? Are you all right?"

"We're three hours from where I intend to leave you," I say, standing, trying to steady my voice, reaching for that gruff façade I used to muster in the first days of his captivity. The sun's just risen; bright light slants over the snow-smothered windshield, diffusing through the van. I dress, shivering violently. "When we get there, I've got to gag you with that ball again. I know it hurts your jaw, but I need to be sure that you don't manage to get help before I'm long gone, okay?"

"You're going to leave me bound? How'm I going to get loose? I don't want to freeze to death." Rob's breath rises in a cloud.

"You'll see. You'll be fine, I promise. Want some breakfast first? Need to piss?"

Rob nods. After we use the piss-can, I pop open a can of Vienna sausages. We lie side by side on the mattress; I feed him with my fingers; we chew in silence. Outside a cardinal is cheering; chickadees are arguing. After our makeshift breakfast, I dress Rob's shaking nakedness in the sweats and socks. I'm about to gag him again—rip of duct tape, sharp in the morning quiet—when he shakes his head.

"Wait, okay? I need to ask you something."

"What is it, kid?"

"So, will we get to talk again?"

"Yes. Before I leave you in the place I have planned."

"O-okay. So we'll never meet again? I'll never see your face?"

"Nope. That would all be unwise on my part, obviously."

"Even if I swear...that I'd never...? Okay. Yeah. Makes sense. Go ahead. I want to get home." Rob's swollen lips are trembling. I kiss him before applying the tape and the hogtie tether.

Not much left to do. Scrape the windshield; clear my vision; let the light in; start the van. It fishtails a little bit in the snow and mud. For a second I think we're stuck, but then the wheels gain traction, and soon we've left behind the pine grove, the place where we lay together for the last time.

chapter forty

THE BARN'S ABANDONED, isolated, set in a snow-crusted field near a stand of leafless locusts. It's a mile from a back road gas station.

I leave Rob in the van. Inside the barn, it takes me only minutes to arrange things the way I want: spread the blanket, set out the food, hang up the key.

Now I cut Rob's feet loose, cuff his hands behind him, help him from the back of the van, and lead him into the trees to relieve himself. The sun's disappeared again, behind clotted clouds, and light snow's begun, drifting like goose down from the Nebraska sky. Now I guide his limping blindness across clumps of dead field grass and into the barn. There I help him sit on the blanket I've spread over the straw-strewn floor. I slip on my mask before unwrapping the feet of tape over his eyes.

After so many sightless hours sunk in darkness, he blinks and squints at me, obviously stunned by the light, even these dim, snow-dulled beams that slant through the otherwise shadowy barn. Gently I pull the tape off his mouth.

"Here," I say, giving him a sip of bottled water. "Look here now, boy." I point to two paper bags I've left on the floor near him. In one are wrapped sandwiches, one pimiento, one baloney; in the other is the book of Shakespeare's sonnets.

"A little lunch for when you get free. No fingerprints on the wrap, by the way. I've used gloves. There's also a little farewell gift. And look over there." I point to a support post on the far side of the barn. "Do you see it? The key?"

Rob peers, eyes watering with strain. "No. I can't see very well yet, dude. I've been pretty much blind for days. Going to take a while to see clearly again."

"That post there. You can see that, right? With those old riding reins hung on it? Directly beneath those reins is a handcuff key. I've hung it on a nail about two feet from the ground. I'm going to leave you here gagged and hogtied. By the time you wriggle across the barn and manage to retrieve that key, I'll be long gone."

"Yeah. Okay. But where am I? How do I get home?"

"Easy. Once you're loose, head out that door there. See it? Just across that field, you'll run into a road. Turn right when you get to it. Maybe you can even hail a car—well, to be honest, I don't know if anyone would pick you up. What with the shoelessness, scruffy sweats, and scruffier face, you look like an escapee from a lunatic asylum. At any rate, soon you'll reach a gas station. From there, you can call your father. And the police. Got it? You'll be fine. Freezing, and with sore feet, I suspect, but, in the long run, fine. And free."

"I don't think I'll ever be free." Rob blinks at me and clears his throat. "So this is goodbye, huh, dude?"

"Yes," I say. I clear my throat too. My damned eyes are moistening up. "So," I say, pulling the rubber ball from my jacket pocket. "Goodbye, son."

"I owe you everything," Rob says. He opens his mouth. I push the ball between his teeth and wrap tape over his lips and about his head. I roll him onto his belly, fold his legs up, cross and tape his ankles, then rope them behind him to his cuffed hands, making of his lean youth a trussed triangle, a circuit of helplessness. It'll take him a good while to make his way across the barn and over to the key.

I stand. Rob grunts, rolling over onto his side. He tugs at his bonds, testing them. He gazes up at me. The look in his wet blue eyes is impossible to define.

I drop onto my knees beside him. Bending, I kiss his forehead. Then—on a whim, without forethought or planning or any care for consequence—I remove my mask.

Beneath the tape, around the ball, Rob emits a little gasp. I kiss his brow again; I chuck his bearded chin. Then I stand. I turn my back on him and briskly head back to the van. I wipe my eyes, warm up the engine, turn up the heater, and drive away, over the rutted road that leads me back to Jay.

TWO

Publish my name and hang up my picture as that of the tenderest lover.

—Walt Whitman

chapter forty-one

THE LILACS ARE cool and wet against my face. Who knows who planted them or how long ago? There was a house here once—you can tell by the remains of the chimney, the apple tree blooming by what's left of a fencerow, and these fragrant lilac bushes by my trailer.

Water beads on the brim of my baseball cap. It's a showery Sunday, late afternoon, chilly for April in the Smokies. The fog's moved in, so thick that all I can see are fuzzy gray and innumerable tree trunks, most of them the straight boles of old tulip trees, their boughs beginning to sprout gold-green leaves. As high as I am on Driggers Knob, I'm in the clouds much of the time. The road leading up here from the valley would terrify visitors—narrow, winding, with sheer drops, sometimes on both sides—but I never get guests.

The rain's coming down harder now, so I hurry up onto the porch and into the trailer, bags of groceries in both hands. I don't cook much anymore—it's just not worth the trouble when you live alone—but today's gloomy weather has made me hungry for chicken and dumplings. That was one of Jay's favorite meals, and it's still one of those dinners that make me feel like a cared-for child, even if it's me caring for myself.

The fat silver tabby, Logan, pads down the hall to greet me, followed closely by his buddy, the fat orange tabby, Angus. After years of living alone, I've learned to survive without human affection, but I do appreciate theirs. I put the groceries away, pop open a beer, and sit for a few minutes, stroking them while they climb over my lap and vie for my attentions.

I'm on my second Bud Light, half-asleep, stretched out beneath an afghan on the couch while the chicken's poaching, when I hear, beneath the drum of rain on the roof, the rumble of a car over gravel, climbing the mountain. Unusual. The only other people who live on Driggers Knob are a young couple with kids who live a mile below me and who have no reason to come up the hill this far, and a middle-aged woman who lives farther up the mountain, who always stays at home on Sundays. The grating sound grows, getting closer. When I rise, displacing the nesting cats, and peer out the window, I see a Jeep pulling into my fog-dim, dusk-dim driveway.

I check my pistol—loaded—and slip it into my pocket. Then I open the door and stare through the screen into the sheets of rain. The Jeep's driver door opens, and a man steps out. He's wearing a cowboy hat, a denim jacket, and mud-streaked chinos; he's strongly built. The fog's too thick to see his face. He takes a few steps, almost slips in the mud, rights himself, and limps toward the porch.

"What do you want?" I shout, sounding deliberately hostile. There's some crazy trash in this county; I've learned to trust no one. Can't be too careful. As wild and sparsely inhabited as this mountain is, anything could happen. I pat the pistol in my pocket, ready to drive the fucker off if necessary.

The man stops, halfway up the stairs, and lifts his head. He tips back his hat, squints up at me, and says, "Al?"

No one's called me that since I left that barn in Nebraska eight years ago. I flip on the porch light. The stranger takes a step back and lifts his cowboy hat off despite the downpour. Rob Drake is standing there. He gives me a faint smile. "Can I come in? It's really coming down out here."

I grip the gun and stare at him. Sweat pops out on my temples.

"I'm alone," he says, giving a wave, a clumsy movement that leads me to believe he's drunk. "No SWAT teams, dude. Just me."

Without a word, I push open the screen. Rob limps up the stairs; I step aside; he enters, scraping muddy cowboy boots on the mat. The cats scatter, fleeing down the hall to the bedroom.

I close the door and lock it. I swipe sweat-beads off my temples and return the pistol to its customary drawer. Then I turn. Rob hangs his hat on the coat rack before pulling a bottle of bourbon from a pocket, placing it on the counter, and shrugging off his jacket.

"Belated housewarming gift," he says, swaying a little. He's wearing a black T-shirt; I can't help but take a quick, hungry look at the thick arms and big chest the tight fabric displays. When he offers his hand, I grasp it. We stand, studying one another, palms pressed together, while the storm batters the trailer's roof, making the same music it did so long ago, on the roof of that ramshackle house up that Virginia cove.

He's not the same, of course, after all these years apart. The most obvious change: there's a jagged white scar snaking over his right cheek. Below that scar, his beard's full, almost bushy, with a flash of gray on the chin. Instead of the buzz-cut I remember, his hair is thick, mussed, with long bangs rain-plastered to his brow. He's wearing glasses, the ugly horn-rimmed kind young men find fashionable these days. He's filled out, no longer that lean gymnast that Jay and I drugged on the jogging trail. His frame's thicker, more muscular, a man's body. There's not much boy left, other than that infectious smile.

"Mind if I sit down?" Without waiting for a reply, he releases my hand, limps to the couch, and sits heavily. Something's wrong with his body, something damaged. He smiles again, gesturing to the beer can I left on the coffee table. "I'm already drunk. Took a six-pack to get me up here. I've been staying at a hotel in Asheville for two days, trying to get up the guts to...well, here I am, and I'm thirsty. Mind if I have one? We can break into your gift later. It's Maker's Mark. I remember you liked that brand. Got some lemons? We could have whiskey sours like you made for us before."

"I have lemons," I say, fetching us two Bud Lights. I sit at one end of the couch; he leans back against the other. We each take a big gulp. My legs are shaking, as are my hands. I tense my thighs, clench my hands into fists, then go limp, willing myself to relax.

Rob gazes at me steadily. "You look great, Al. Your beard's grayer, but you've lost weight."

I clear my throat. I speak slowly, trying to sound composed. "I don't cook much anymore. I hate to cook for one."

"But you're cooking now, aren't you? What you got going over there on the stove?"

"Chicken and dumplings."

"Mind if I stay for dinner?"

"You're acting like we're frat brothers who haven't seen one another since college. Guys at a high school reunion."

"Yes, I am." Rob takes a long swig. "Mind if I stay for dinner? I remember how good a cook you are. No one ever cooked for me like that except for my mom."

"I'm not letting you drive back down this mountain, as drunk as you are, so, yes, stay to dinner. How did you find me?"

"Things you let slip. Back then, stupid as I was, back when I thought I was going to be the hottest new detective around..."

"You're not a detective?"

"God, no."

"A cop?"

"God, no. I teach English at a community college. Or did. I took a semester off to make sense of things. Well, to be honest, I was, uh, politely asked to take some time off. I've been a little erratic lately."

"English? How'd that happen?"

"It happened on your couch, actually. With all that tape over my eyes, and my hands and feet tied, I had a lot of time to think hard about my life, especially since I was afraid I'd never get away alive. Remember how I told you I liked poetry? How my father used to make fun of me for it? Well, blinded as I was, still I started to see a lot. How I was into law enforcement only because my father was. So when I got home—Man, it pissed my dad off! We didn't speak for six months!—I went back to school and got a teaching degree with a specialization in English and creative writing."

Rob shakes his head and grins. "Well, back to my brief career as Sherlock Holmes and how I found you. When I was your hostage, when I was blinded, I guess my hearing got sharper, or I caught things I would otherwise have ignored. Once you called Jay 'Jeff.' You talked about his friend Zac dying of AIDS. You said something about having heard a lot about prison. It was clear you two hadn't asked for a ransom. And I heard Jay ranting about my father on your phone." Rob wipes beer foam from his moustache with the back of his hand. "It took a while for me to piece it together. For a long time I'd tried to forget all of it. But then I had reason to remember."

"And what you figured out you kept to yourself, it seems. Otherwise, Jay and I would have been arrested long ago."

"Yes." Rob leans back, takes another swig of beer, and closes his eyes. "So your real name is Mark? All right if I still call you Al?"

"Sure," I say. "Allen's my middle name." My heartbeat's hammering my throat. I swallow hard, trying to calm down. Rising, I check the chicken, find it good and done, and fish it from the broth to cool.

"It'll be a while till dinner's ready. You want some cheese and crackers?"

Rob tips up his spectacles and rubs his eyes. His stomach growls. "That'd be great. I haven't eaten much today. Too nervous."

I fetch Saltines and slice Cheddar. We snack. "First time we've eaten together that you didn't have to feed me," Rob says matter-of-factly. The cats slink down the hall, stare at the stranger, sit at a safe distance, and study him.

In between bites, Rob reaches over and pats my shoulder. "I'm sorry about Jay. Jeff, that is."

"Thanks," I sigh.

"Were you two still together when he died?"

"Oh, yes. But by the time of the accident—that was nearly a year and a half after you...after you and I parted—by then most of what was between Jeff and me...well, there wasn't much left. He got too involved in the drug scene, too attached to his chemical highs, to have much room for me, plus he never quite forgave me for—"

"For saving me?"

"Yes. I lost track of the number of times he accused me of choosing you over him. Our relationship never really recovered from that."

"Damn." Rob pats my shoulder again, then squeezes it. "I'm really sorry. Shit."

"Not your fault. It's not as if you asked to be kidnapped. He and I escaped any legal consequences, but I guess we paid for that crime in other ways."

"What happened when you returned to Virginia? After you drove me back to Nebraska?"

"Jeff was high as hell when I got back to the cove. We got into a knock-down/drag-out fistfight I still have nightmares about. Basically beat the shit out of each other."

"Was he drugged up the night he died?"

"Yep. Crystal meth."

"So...what happened that night? If you don't mind talking about it."

"I don't mind. It's been long years ago, though, yeah, it also seems like last week. Jeff was always hot-tempered, but after you left, after he'd graduated from booze to drugs, he got much worse. We fought constantly—verbally, for the most part, but sometimes physically. We had another horrible argument the evening he died."

"An argument? Over me?" Rob leans back and takes a lengthy swig of beer.

"Over you, yes. And over all sorts of other things." Bowing my head, I nibble at a Saltine. "Our dwindling sex life. Our finances. His drug use. You know how resentments can build up between two people."

"Oh, yes, I sure do." Rob makes a wry face. "Fortress walls made of heaped shit and topped with barbed wire."

"Well put. Jeff threw a beer mug against the floor and told me he was going to drive around a little to cool down. Never came back. A cop knocked on the door about five in the morning, told me Jeff had driven his truck into a tree."

"Was that an accident, do you think, or did he do it on purpose?"

"An accident, I think. It was rainy that night; the roads were slick. I'll never know for sure. And I'll never forgive myself." I finish my beer and stand. "Want another? This somber talk is making me thirsty."

"Hell, yes. Please. Mind if I take off my boots?"

"No problem. Make yourself comfortable. Get under that afghan if you're chilly."

"You always knew how to make me feel cozy, even when you had me bound up." Rob grins thinly, tugging off his boots. "Jay—Jeff, I mean—Jeff, on the other hand, he was damned mean to me, and I hated him for a long time. Used to dream about beating his face in. Till I learned all that I did about him. How many times he'd been admitted to the prison hospital."

"Yes," I say, fetching two more Bud Lights from the fridge. "Jeff was a good-looking guy. He was big and strong, but in prison there were men who were bigger and stronger. He told me he was gang-raped in the shower and in guys' cells so many times he lost count. It was a miracle that he didn't end up with AIDS like his cell-mate Zac."

I set Rob up with a beer before striding into the kitchen to begin the process of picking apart the chicken. It's still so hot it burns my fingers. "Booze had always been enough to help him forget. But then... I think that's the reason he started doing drugs right after we took you. He thought that abducting you, raping you, would help him feel like he was avenging himself—"

"On my father." Rob stretches out on the couch, props his head on a pillow, and closes his eyes.

"Yes. But instead I think it all just brought back..."

"Yeah. I get it. I remember that time he drugged me before he fucked me, how he cried and said, 'I know how you feel, boy.' And you helped him kidnap me because you loved him. And because you loved me. Right?"

"Yes." I finish shredding the chicken breasts; now I start shredding the leg-meat. It's good to have a task to focus on.

"And did you still love him when he died?"

"Yes. As fucked-up and distant and drugged-out as he was, I still loved him."

"And do you still love me?"

"Is that why you tracked me down?" I turn, glaring at my handsome guest—blue eyes, messy hair, beefy torso swelling beneath his shirt. It seems hard to believe that he could be more desirable than he was those many years ago, but he is, even with a scarred face. "To ask me that? Is that why you're here?"

"I don't know why I'm here," Rob whispers, pulling the afghan over him. "But it's good to see you. You've got a cozy little eyrie here."

We're silent for a time. Rob rolls on his side, buries his face in the pillow, and dozes, starting up a light snore. For a full minute I watch him sleep, finally pulling my eyes away with great effort. Every beautiful detail's a threat. Haven't I been clean and cold too long to let him in?

I finish shredding the chicken and start mixing batter for the dumplings. The silver tabby, deciding that Rob's harmless, jumps onto the couch, sniffs him, climbs onto his hip, curls up, and falls asleep.

The chicken broth's re-achieved a slow simmer when Rob snorts. "Al? Al?" He bolts upright, peering anxiously around. The tabby, unseated, hops onto the floor and finds a new napping nook beneath the coffee table.

"Shit. Another bad dream. Sorry I fell asleep," he says, yawning. "I'm really exhausted. Haven't been sleeping well lately."

"This'll all be ready in about fifteen minutes," I say.

"Mind if we drink a little more first?" Rob says, tipping back the last of his can. "I think we have a little more catching up to do. How about you break open that Maker's Mark and we have those whiskey sours? For old time's sake?"

"Haven't you had enough?"

"No. No, dude. Not by a long shot. I got my own demons to dull, y'know?"

I pour whiskey, squeeze lemons, add sugar, stir, add ice. We sit side by side on the couch again. Rob takes a big sip and smacks his lips. "Ahh. Yeahhh. You do these up right."

"Looks like you've gotten as fond of liquor as Jay was," I say.

"Yeah. Well, you introduced me to some tasty drinks—not to mention those great redneck meals—and then, well, when I got home, I had a few things to forget myself."

"Still, I guess congratulations are in order," I say, clinking his glass with mine. "You moved on despite your ordeal. You found happiness, right?"

"Happiness? What?"

"Your wedding. After I left you in the barn, I kept track of you online. The articles about your reappearance, the story you told the cops, the investigation, the unsolved case."

"The pact, dude. The pact." Rob gives my arm a soft punch. "After all you'd done for me—you saved my life, Al!—I wasn't going to tell them much. At that point I hadn't figured anything out anyway. About how to track you down."

"I figured Jay and I were in the clear when, after a solid month, the cops still hadn't knocked down the door. Then I read about your marriage. To Sarah. That's when I decided that, well, it wasn't doing me any good to read about your happiness online, especially since my own life was going to hell, so I stopped my Internet research. I tried to put you behind me. You haunted me, Rob."

"Haunted? Well, dude, that makes two of us. So you don't know I'm divorced." Rob gives me a crooked grin and takes a long sip. "*Damned* good drink."

"What? Divorced? No, I didn't know that."

Rob chuckles. "Long story short. I was pretty screwed up for a while when I got home. I didn't know how to feel, about myself, about what had happened to me. You fucked things up, you know? Not just kidnapping me, but being kind to me. Making love to me. Saving my life. I didn't know how to feel. Sarah was so hysterical with thanks to have me back, I thought it was going to get better between us. She ended up pregnant; we got married, but then she lost the kid. Still, she and I got along all right, in a half-assed way, for a couple of years, though the sex dwindled down to next to nothing after she miscarried. She'd just lie there, you know? And half the time I couldn't get it up. Then I told her the truth."

"What truth?"

"That I'd...that Jay had raped me. I didn't have the guts to tell her that you and I, that I'd enjoyed...the way you touched me. God knows what she would have done if she'd known that. As it was..." Rob puts his drink down, rests his elbows on his knees, and laughs.

"What? None of this sounds funny to me."

"In retrospect, dude. In retrospect. We'd pulled into a Cracker Barrel parking lot, and I saw someone who looked like you—big, burly guy with a black beard—and that reminded me of all that'd happened, and...like a big pussy, I started to cry. And for some fucking reason I don't know to this day, I told her about the rapes. And do you know what she did?"

"What? I have no idea."

"She puked, dude! She *puked*. All across the dashboard of my car. And after that, it was like I was shamed, unmanned in her eyes. A fucking steer, you know? Ball-less! It was never the same. She wouldn't even touch me. And still I hung on, I guess because I was so fucking afraid to be alone. But when she asked me for a divorce a year later, I was almost relieved."

Rob seizes his whiskey sour, gulps the remainder, and slams the glass on the coffee table so hard my drink gives a little hop. "Ump, sorry, I'm a little high-strung these days. So anyway, my bike accident was right after that. I'd signed the divorce papers. I was wishing I'd never told her what I did. I was wishing she was as kind as you were. I was wishing I could find someone who touched me as tenderly as you did, as...intensely. Shit. Oh, shit. I'm so pathetic."

Rob roughly rubs his temples with both hands. "Damn, my head hurts. I get these headaches sometimes, ever since the accident. So it was raining that night, and I'd had a few beers, so I guess I was slower than usual, my reflexes, you know, and some son of a bitch—I was driving through a little crossroads in southern Nebraska—he didn't see me, I guess, hit and run, so I ended up in a ditch, face and leg all torn up, my Harley absolutely totaled. That's how I got this." Rob runs a hand over his scarred cheek. "And my vision's never been the same." He taps his glasses. "And I got a hitch in my get-along now." Rob pats his right thigh. "Poor ole crip. This rain makes me ache. Hey, I'm starved, dude. Let's eat. That chicken smells great!"

chapter forty-two

"FULL AS A tick, isn't that what you hillbillies say?" Rob pats his belly, unbuckles his belt, and collapses on the couch. "If you make me one last whiskey sour and let me spend the night, I'll do those dishes in the morning."

We've each devoured two big bowls of chicken and dumplings, followed by the last of some store-bought pecan pie. The cats have entirely acclimated to my guest, climbing all over him, demanding love and back scratches.

"Only one more," I say, mixing drinks. "You're drunk enough."

Rob gives me a wink when I hand him the tumbler. "I need to be drunk tonight. I'm pretty damned nervous. Scared shitless, actually."

"You're scared? What about me? It's not like the statute of limitation's run out on your kidnapping."

Rob grabs my arm. "There was no kidnapping. Sit down here with me."

When I do, he says, "Can I put my head in your lap? Like we did before?" There's that little boy's voice I remember, deep but full of a barely suppressed pleading.

"Sure. I guess," I say, through my uncertainty, surprise, and confusion. Suddenly I'm terrified of touching him, afraid of what might happen if I feel his warmth against me. I've tried to forget him for so many years, but, in his presence, all those heaped-up attempts at amnesia are breaking apart like an earthen dam. The lines of his body have changed, but still he makes me ache.

"Thanks." He stretches out, resting his head in my lap with a deep sigh. I cover his solid frame with the afghan. The silver tabby immediately repositions himself on my guest's belly. Rob and I gaze at one another, take sips of our drinks, and gaze some more.

"You've got some gray," I say, tapping his whiskered chin with one tentative finger.

"Getting old."

"Hell, you aren't old. You're only thirty, right? *I'm* old," I say, brushing my own beard. "Talk about going gray."

"Looks great on you. Say, Al? You didn't answer my question."

"What question?"

"Do you still love me?"

"I'll answer that if you tell me why you're here."

Rob closes his eyes. "Because...after Sarah, I slept around some, a bunch of chicks, even dated a few, but none of it helped. Then I hit a few gay bars in Lincoln, slept with a few guys, sucked a few cocks. Guess I really am bi. But none of it was any good, no one touched me like..."

Rob opens his eyes, bites his lip, then clenches his eyes shut once more. "And I kept having nightmares. Of Jay hurting me. I'm still scarred, by the way. My chest. And I kept having dreams about you, fantasies too. Even when I was still with Sarah, I'd be jacking off in the shower, thinking about you tying me up, stuffing your dick in my mouth or taking me from behind. After the divorce, I'd see some big bearded guy like you in a bar and try to pick him up. But those men were never..."

Rob takes a deep breath. "Or I'd be in some damn diner, munching on a hot dog, or getting fat"—he slaps his belly—"on biscuits and gravy...though, dude, the biscuits were never as good as yours! And I'd think of you. So then, I just got tired of the dreams and tired of being lonely, tired of not knowing what had happened to me or why, so I started doing some research—on my father's career, prison records, Jay's, uh, Jeff's file. Found out he'd died. Finally found the house where you kept me outside of Pulaski. Found the Red Line Diner. Took longer to find out how you fit into the picture. Anyway, my generation's pretty good at computers, so... Here I am."

"I still love you."

Rob opens his eyes. He lifts a hand and cups my cheek. "Really?"

"Yes. What the fuck do I have left to lose? My dignity?" I snort. "I love you. I've tried to forget you for years. I never could. But that doesn't mean I want you here."

"No?" Rob strokes my face. "Why not?"

"Because how could you forgive me for all that happened? How could you love me back? Because why the hell should I open myself up again if..."

I shake my head and rub my forehead. "I lost you. Then I lost Jay. You're like twin spears in my side. I'm happy up here, Rob. I'm happy alone. In the cold clouds. With my cats. With the fog and the forest and the lilac blooms. Working online. Dealing with other human beings only once or twice a week, when I drive into town for groceries. I see clearly when I'm alone. When I'm not fogged in with desire. I don't do stupid things anymore. I'm safe. And the world's safe from me."

"Sounds like you've become a coward."

"What the fuck do you mean by that? Why should I let myself feel for you again? Why should I take such a chance?"

Rob sits up with a jerk. The tabby flees; the afghan hits the floor. He rises to his feet, glowering.

"Like I took a big risk tonight? Driving up here?"

"I'd say. You stupid shit, driving up here drunk. As narrow and twisted as that road is, you could have been killed."

"That's not the risk I'm talking about! Damn you!" Rob snatches his drink from the coffee table, gulps it, and throws the emptied glass against the wall, where it shatters.

"Kidnapping me! And beating me. Holding a knife to my throat. Making me hate you. And then touching me! That fucking unforgettable touch! Your mouth on mine, your mouth on my tits and my cock, your tongue and then your cock up my ass. Spreading me wide; opening me up. You opened me, dude! The things you forced me to feel! I'm ruined! *Ruined*, damn you! Who would want me like this? Scarred-up, fucked-up, neurotic cripple!" Rob shouts, clenching his fists. "Touching me like that, and then risking your life to set me free, so I'd owe you till the goddamn end of time? Showing me your face, and then turning your back and leaving me there with a fucking book of love poems in the fucking heart of winter?"

Rob turns his back on me. "It's been the heart of winter ever since, don't you get it? 'Too dear for my possessing?' No *shit*! Expecting me to forget! You fucker! I should kick your ass!"

My throat's so tight I can barely speak. "Do you think I've ever forgiven myself? I'm so sorry. You need to sober up and go home, Rob. Punch me, and then head on down the hill. There's nothing for you here."

Rob faces me again. His bearded cheeks are tear-streaked. He falls to his knees by the couch; his head falls heavily onto my lap; his arms clasp my legs. I sit stiffly, still afraid to touch him.

"I used to read those sonnets you left me with and wonder what had happened to you, where you were. 'Thy sweet love remembered such wealth brings, / That then I scorn to change my state with kings.' That's the line that used to go through my head when I lay beside Sarah, after we'd tried to make love and failed."

My hands are shaking. They need a solid rest. I rest them on Rob's head.

He pauses, then hugs my legs harder. "No one—not Sarah, not the little bitches I knew before her, not the little bitches and cocksure, self-absorbed studs I've known since—none of them touched me and moved me like you have. That's why I'm here. I want to see if, during all those years we've been apart, I just dreamed it up. Just imagined how you made love to me. How you held me. How...passionate you were. You treated me with more fervor and more kindness than anyone ever has. That's what I remember. I need to find out if I remembered wrong, if I made it all up, fantasized it, how you made me feel. If I remembered wrong, I'm free. If not..."

Rob gets stiffly to his feet. He slips off his glasses and puts them on the coffee table. Then he pulls off his T-shirt. His chest and belly are still pale, but mature now, the brawny curves dusted with sparse brown hair. There's the X Jay made, the lingering ridges of cruelty, perpendicular scars across his torso. The six-pack is gone; he sports the slightest bulge of a beer-gut, a hint of love handles. Now Rob drops his chinos, then his briefs, and steps out of them. The musk of his nakedness washes over me. He stands there, clad in nothing but athletic socks, his cock lengthening. An ugly scar runs from the middle of his furry right thigh down over his knee, streaking his calf.

"Touch me, Al. Please? Please?" he says, deep voice suddenly shaky. "No one's touched me in months." His blue eyes scorch me—desperate, half-crazed—then his head droops, his glance drops to my feet. "I know I'm not built like I was before. I'm not as...hot? Desirable? Shit, I drink and eat too much; I've got to find comfort somewhere. I lift, but I haven't done gymnastics in years. You're the only one...who'd want me. Do you still want me?"

I stand. "God, yes." I grasp Rob's hands, and then I pull him to me. He locks his arms around my back and breaks down, crying against my shoulder. Not the half-suppressed sobs of a man trying his best to hold back, but the out-and-out weeping of a man without shame, who knows he's safe, in the presence of someone who understands sorrow. His naked body is solid and warm, pressing frantically against mine.

"Come on," I say, leading him down the hall to the bedroom, where a dim lamp glows. The room's small, crammed with bookshelves, leaving just enough space for the mattress. We sit on the edge of the bed, and Rob keeps sobbing. I kiss his forehead, wrap my arms around him, and hug him till my elbows ache.

The violence of his crying tapers off slowly, ending with sniffles and cussing. "Shit. Oh, shit. I'm done," he gasps, wiping his face with the back of one hand. "Shit, I'm sorry. I'm really drunk. I've been holding all that back for a long time. You got a Kleenex?"

"Right here," I say, pulling one from the box by the bed. He grabs it and blows his nose. "Damn. Snotty feeb. Now my head hurts even worse."

"Stretch out," I say. I pull back the blankets and help him slide beneath them. I sit beside him, stroking his wet face. He looks up at me, eyes sad and tired.

"Quite the beard," I say, running my fingers through it.

"Please. Please, Al. Can I stay here?" Rob takes my hand and kisses it. "Please?"

"Of course. You're too drunk to drive." Clicking off the lamp, I rise.

"Where are you going?"

"You need your sleep. I'm going to camp out on the couch."

Rob snorts. "You're a crazy man. Get naked and get in here with me. I'm so sad I'm about ready to cry again. Or drive my Jeep into the side of this mountain. Get in here and hold me, dude."

"I don't know how wise—"

"Wise? Fuck wise. Get in here. Please, Al. I'm not asking you to fuck me, at least not yet. I'm asking you to hold me all night. I'm so starved for touch, touch that...means something, I'm ready to shatter."

I strip and slide in beside Rob. His bare hip's hot against mine. The cats immediately join us, leaping onto the bed, settling about our feet.

"I'm not used to sleeping with someone else," I admit, wrapping an arm around Rob and pulling him close. "I've been pretty much celibate since Jay died. Fucking around, trawling the Internet...there just didn't seem to be any point to it."

Rob rolls onto his side, resting his head on my chest and an arm across my belly. "Yeah, I understand." He gives a soft laugh. "Your skills would be wasted on strangers. This feels good, though. Doesn't it? Doesn't it?" He nuzzles me with his beard. "Oh, God, it feels good."

"I've dreamed of this for nearly a decade. Of course it feels good. It feels wonderful. Have you really forgiven me?"

"Yes. Have you forgiven me? I mean, it sounds like my presence was what put Jay over the edge."

"He'd been veering closer and closer to that edge for years. It's not your fault. We took you, remember? It's not as if you connived to seduce me."

Rob rolls over, his back to me. "Spoon?" he says simply. I oblige him, slipping an arm beneath his head, wrapping another around his chest, pulling him tightly against my torso.

"Oh, God, Al. Oh, God. Yes. Just being in your bed, in your arms, makes me feel... so cared for. It's just like I remembered. I didn't dream any of it. It was all real. Al?"

"Yep?" I kiss his head; his thick hair smells like grass.

"When I asked if I could stay here, I didn't just mean tonight. I've looked for you for months. Got a semester's leave from my job. I'd like to...stay with you for awhile. See how... things feel."

"Rob, we don't even know one another." My fingers trace the scars across his chest, tweak a nipple, and dip into his navel.

"Buuuulll-shit. Who do you know better than me?"

No need to search my mind. I know the answer to that. "No one."

"I thought so. You've made yourself a hermit. Guess I don't blame you. I've kind of done the same." Rob scoots even closer, his butt nestling against my groin.

"I'm not in the market for a roommate, much less a lover, a partner." Even as I speak, I can feel my cock hardening against his rump.

"So you want me to leave tomorrow and not come back? You don't want to wake up with me in your bed? You don't want to make love to me? Am I that fat and scarred-up? Damaged goods?"

"Bastard," I say, squeezing a handful of pec-flesh. "Can't you feel my dick stiffening against you? I think you're even more beautiful now." I stroke his scarred cheek, and then I kiss it. "You're a man, not a boy. And we're all damaged."

"Are you going to make love to me?"

"Not tonight. Too soon. And you're too drunk."

"Are you going to let me stay here?"

"For how long?"

"For as long as you want me to stay."

"Yes."

"Are you going to make love to me tomorrow? Are you going to fuck me?"

"I don't know. Maybe. Probably." I squeeze his chest again, then a butt cheek. "Yes. If you want me to. Do you want me to?"

"I think so. Shit, who do I think I'm kidding? Yes. *Hell*, yes. Take it slow. But, yes."

"I'll probably tie you up. Not because I need to but because that will turn me on even more. Your powerlessness always got me hard. That all right with you?"

"Sure, dude. Rope me and ride me. Whatever pleases you, Daddy."

"Daddy? Ha! Hot. Keep that up."

Rob nudges his butt against my cock and snickers. "Whatever you say, Daddy."

"You've become quite the tease, haven't you? Look, Rob, it won't be as intense as you recall. You thought you were going to die, remember? When you asked me to make love to you."

"I know. But it'll be wonderful nevertheless. I want to feel you...inside me again. I want your loads...in my mouth, and up my ass. Will you make me biscuits tomorrow? With sausage gravy? Like you did before?"

"No buttermilk."

"What if I drive into town in the morning and buy you some?"

"Long drive. Nearly ten miles."

"Worth the drive."

"Yes, I'll make you biscuits and gravy. Do you love me, Rob?"

"I don't think I've ever loved anyone before. Except my mother. I thought I loved Sarah. But she didn't haunt me when she left, didn't make me ache. Like you did. I think about your body, about you on top of me, inside me. I think about you touching me...rough and tender. About you feeding me, holding me, keeping me warm, making me feel safe and cared for. Like this. Like this here now, lying here together, after so many years alone, with your arms around me. Feels like home."

"You feel all that? Really?"

"Why would I lie, dude?"

"Sounds like love to me."

"Yeah? Guess so." Rob lifts my hand from his chest and kisses it, the back of it, and then the palm. Then he places it over his heart. I cup his pec. I play with the fine hair rimming the nipple, the light coating of fur.

"Sweet," Rob whispers. He sighs, buries his face in the pillow, and begins to snore. I lie there in the dark, feeling his heartbeat against my hand. Outside, fog's swathing the forest, rain's soaking the black earth and, along bough and twig tip, a new year's unfurling its green-gold. Spring's seething over the mountains, a shift so slow it's imperceptible. Something similar's shifting inside me: hope, a tenderness I thought I'd never know again. I kiss Rob's shoulder, sink my face in his shaggy hair, breathe in his musky smell, and close my eyes.

We sleep close and we sleep soundly. Gray dawn-light wakes me, and hard rain drumming the roof. Something in the melancholy sound makes me think of Jay, his last moments, that tree rising up before him, the red impact. I think of his grave, rain's fingers sliding over his ashes. I think of that cold house in the cove, that young captive: his white skin like sculpture, those strips of silvery tape, his cries for help, his wet blue eyes. I took him, and then he took me. I'm the captive now, I think. Bound to that lost boy and now to this lost man beside me.

I stroke Rob's scarred cheek. His eyes flicker open.

"Al? Where you going, Daddy?" he whimpers, grabbing my hand. "Don't go."

"I'm here. I'm not going anywhere. Too early to get up," I say. "How'd you sleep?"

"Great," Rob murmurs. "No bad dreams. Thanks for letting me stay. I'm so glad I'm here."

"Me too. Let's stay in bed and cuddle for a few hours. Then we can head down the hill together. Get buttermilk for those biscuits you want. Maybe fetch some cube steak too. Have country-fried steak for dinner. How's that sound? With mashed potatoes, pepper gravy, and green beans."

"Man, I'm going to get fat if I stay here. Fat, fat, fat." Rob wraps his arms around my waist, presses his face into my chest hair, and closes his eyes. In a bit I'll get up, feed the cats, and make coffee. Right now, I'm going to lie here, listen to spring rain on the roof, savor the warmth, and watch my lover sleep.

about the author

JEFF MANN grew up in Covington, Virginia, and Hinton, West Virginia, receiving degrees in English and forestry from West Virginia University. His poetry, fiction, and essays on being a Southerner, and so at the edge of the gay community, and the appeal of leather bars and bear culture have appeared in many publications, including *Best Gay Stories*, *The Gay and Lesbian Review Worldwide*, *Best Gay Erotica*, *Bloom*, *Appalachian Heritage*, and *Tales from the Den*. He teaches creative writing at Virginia Tech in Blacksburg, Virginia.

CPSIA information can be obtained at www.ICGtesting.com
Printed in the USA
LVOW06s1155230815

451200LV00008B/694/P